# Tom and Chris and the blind monk

A tale of ghostly goings on at Netley Abbey

A debut novel by Eliot Easterby.
Find my short stories on Amazon.co.uk.

## Chapter One

Brother Peter knew he was going to die. No matter what he said or did, he knew the Abbot was going to kill him.

He had thought that life as a monk was going to be a peaceful existence of prayer and farming and helping the local community.

From day one at the Abbey he had discovered the opposite. The residents of Netley lived in terror of the monks. The monks ruled the village by fear. Fear of eternal damnation for not supporting the Abbey and paying its tithes, but also fear of physical violence, meted out in the dead of night by the Abbots enforcers.

Peter had tried to moderate the worst excesses of the Abbey. Rending genuine assistance to many poorer members of the community and speaking out to the other monks during meal and recreation times, questioning the way the Abbey operated.

Two nights later he was rudely awakened as a hessian sack was pulled over his head. Three bodies held him down, while a forth tied the bag in place. They then proceeded to beat him with sticks until he passed out and was unable to defend himself.

Peter regained consciousness long after breakfast the following day, with welts the size of crab apples on his arms and legs and multi-coloured bruising over most of his body.

Peter was taken to the infirmary, where he was treated with kindness and care, but no one seemed to have any idea how or why his beating had occurred.

The Abbot came to see Peter and spoke words of sympathy and kindness. He claimed he had already started an investigation. The Abbots eyes told a different story. He only made eye contact when he began to talk about God's plan for Peter and how any misfortune Peter had suffered was a result of him veering from God's plan.

Peter knew revenge was ungodly and unseemly for a monk, but he also believed that the greedy Abbot should be punished for his behaviour.

Whilst recovering, Peter hatched a plan. He would try to fit in. He would work with the Abbot. He would do as he was told. He would collect the monies he was told to collect, no matter how outrageous the demands, but all the time he would watch and listen and find where the Abbot kept his wealth and discover all the means he used to accrue it.

The majority of the monks lived simple lives of prayer with few possessions. In each cell would be a mattress made of hay and whatever other possessions the Abbot allowed.

Whilst an acolyte in Beaulieu (Be-yew-lee) Abbey he had learnt; no one may presume to give, receive or retain anything of his own, nothing at all - not a hook, writing tablet or stylus - in short, not a single item, especially since monks may not have free disposal of even their own bodies and wills. For their needs they are to look to the father of the monastery and are not allowed anything which the Abbot has not given or permitted. All things should be the common possession of all, as it is written, so that no one presumes to call anything his own.

Peter had his mattress and his plain white woollen Cistercian monks' habit. The Abbot deigned to give him nothing else. During his duties Brother Peter had visited the Abbot's lodge to wait on his holiness. What he saw there, was nothing like the austerity he lived in and nothing like the basic quarters of the Abbot at Beaulieu. Abbot William of Netley Abbey was an extraordinarily fat man who puffed and wheezed as he waddled around. He dripped with gold. Opulent rings and necklaces, strung with gold crosses embossed with gemstones. The Abbot's Lodge was a picture of luxury. A huge double bed piled with silks, velvet and furs. Loungers, curtains, tapestries and rugs adorned the walls and floors. A huge oak table covered with platters of meat, pastries and fruit. A roaring fire in the hearth of every room. Visits to the Abbot's Lodge during the winter months gave a welcome opportunity to defrost his hands.

Peters religious work consisted mainly of copying books of the bible onto new vellum scrolls. When vellum was in short supply, he would be drafted into helping with its production. His other jobs involved chopping wood, tending crops, helping in the kitchen and cleaning.

It was his work in the vellum tanneries that allowed Peter to collect off cuts of vellum, which he bound into a small book. A book which he used to record the sins he saw around him.

He knew the Bishop of Winchester visited the Abbey on a regular basis, usually about twice a year. He had seen the Bishop during his first week at Netley. The Bishop had read a list of people who had sinned against the church. By the authority of God, father almighty and the blessed virgin Mary and all the Saints he excommunicated, anathematised and delivered over to the devil all the aforesaid malefactors. Peter shuddered at the thought. He feared that if he did nothing to prevent the excesses of the Abbot, that he would be cursed likewise, when the Bishop found out.

So Peter had recorded details of goods smuggled through the Abbey, he recorded tithes charged to the villagers and farmers and what tithe was paid to the church and crown. The Abbot was always pleading poverty and hiding goods and property from the kings inspectors and had recently secured a reduction in taxes, despite the fact that Peter had seen hundreds of gold and thousands of silver coins in a chest at the Abbot's Lodge.

Peters greatest friend and confidant was a nun called Sister Mary.  She was kind and thoughtful and the only other person he had spotted showing outward disapproval of the regime in place.

He had quietly warned her about her behaviour but urged her to help him collect information.  They met in secret on a regular basis and eventually hatched a plan.

The Bishop was visiting in two weeks and Mary had been asked to organise a program for his visit.  That program was to include a guided tour of the vellum works.  A tour to be guided by Brother Peter, where he would raise the subject of smuggling in a discrete way and test the Bishop's response, before revealing the information in his diary.

The day arrived and Peter mentioned that he was worried that some of the villagers may be involved in smuggling and that he feared for their souls. The Bishop's response was that he was sure the Abbot was aware of the problem. Peter had then said, that he thought the Abbot had been aware of the problem for some time.

He was interrupted by an angry response, emphasising how hard working and generous the Abbot was and how lowly Brothers should be very careful how they spoke about their betters. Peter had said no more and swiftly changed the subject.

Peter later learned that, only that morning, the Abbot had gifted a manor house to the Bishop !

A new plan was needed. Clearly, the Bishop was going to be no help. So, in order to save their immortal souls, Peter and Mary, made the fateful decision to take direct action. They decided to steal the Abbots hoard and secretly distribute it to the poor.

The Abbot's lodge had little in the way of security, a few latches and bars, that were rarely used, but then few people would have believed an Abbey had much worth stealing, candlesticks and crosses would be difficult to sell discretely.  Even fewer would have risked eternal damnation.

Sailors, however, were a sinful lot and the nearby towns of Southampton and Portsmouth had plenty of sailors. Occasionally, gangs of sailors would come ashore and steal sheep and chickens from the outlying farms.

  Peter bought a cheap sailor's earring from a stall beside the ferry landing in Woolston, whilst out shopping for the kitchens.  He had no money, but traded it for food from the wagon.  The kitchens would complain about short loads again, but not too loudly.  The earring would be left in the Abbot's Lodge, when the chest was spirited away.
  The Abbey had a drainage channel that ran through the kitchens and latrines.  It was twenty foot deep with stone walls and floor. It was fed from a lake behind the Abbot's Lodge and ran through a tunnel all the way downhill to the shore. A distance of about five hundred paces.  The tunnel was exposed in the kitchens, where a wooden cover could

be removed for disposal of kitchen slops. A wooden seating arrangement was placed over the channel in the latrines.   A third opening was directly behind the Abbot's Lodge.  A lot of waste was generated by the Abbot ! From Autumn to Spring a steady overflow of water from the lake kept the drainage channel fragrant.  During the Summer boards were lifted from the sluice gate every Monday to flush out the excrement.

  It took months of waiting, but eventually, the right opportunity arose.  It was a Tuesday, in August.  The channel had been flushed, the Abbot was away and Mary had been on cleaning duties in the lodge since June.  Peter came to help her with her duties, with a cord tied round his waist, beneath his habit.  The pair of them lowered a chest filled with every gold coin they could find, into the Abbots latrine and dropped the rope in with it.  Twenty feet below in the darkness, it was completely concealed, even during broad daylight.

Later that night.  Long after the last prayer had been said and the fires banked, Peter lit a candle and placed it in his shuttered lantern.

The climb down the kitchen waste hole was simple.  The channel, only three feet wide, could be easily straddled and with a hand and a foot on either side it was a simple matter of bracing yourself against the rough stonework and gradually working your way down, having lowered the lantern first.  Needless to say Peter had stripped to his loin cloth and was barefoot.

He crept along the drainage tunnel using a tiny chink of light from his candle lantern to avoid the worst of the excrement.  Despite his best efforts, he was soon smeared with waste and stinking but he had reached the chest.

It was too heavy to lift on his own, so he dragged it, as slowly as possible, to avoid excessive noise.  It took him over an hour to reach the recess he had previously hollowed in the wall after removing four large stones. He packed earth back in around the chest. Wedged the stones back in place and packed earth tightly in the gaps around the rocks. The remaining earth he spread out across the tunnel floor ready to be washed away by the next flush.

Afterwards, he completed his trip to the shoreline, where he swam in the sea to wash off any evidence of his trip. Peter picked his way stealthily back through the woods to a hole in the hedgerow surrounding the Abbey. He made his way to the vestry door, where he quickly slipped into a clean habit, before making his way back to his cell.

The Abbot's enforcers are looking for him. He had been rudely advised by Brother Francis that he was in deep trouble, he claimed the Abbot had had someone watching him since his talk with the Bishop and now the enforcers had been sent to get him.

Peter knew he was going to die. He knew the Abbot had killed people before and he knew that whatever he said or did he would be killed. So he vowed to say nothing and have his revenge.

Peter made a last entry in his diary and hid it behind the loose rock near the ceiling of his cell.

## Chapter 2

'So, do you reckon he got away with it then.' said Chris. 'Course not.' said Tom. Don't you realise who this is. It's Blind Peter. Skipper told us the story at Scout camp, when we were sat round the fire. Besides, that was the last entry. Don't you think he would have written more if he had survived.'

The story of Blind Peter had featured a greedy monk who had hoarded a treasure until discovered by a virtuous Abbot who demanded that he hand it over to the church, so it could be distributed to the poor. The monk had repeatedly refused and in his anger the Abbot had insisted that if he would not reveal the location of his treasure, then the Church would ensure that he could never receive the benefit of his ill gotten gains. Brother Peter had been strapped to a chair and his eyes burned out with a red hot poker.

Thinking back about the story, Tom had always felt, that this was hardly the expected behaviour from a virtuous man of the cloth, but then he had heard about other medieval punishments for witches and decided that maybe today's standards of behaviour had not applied back then. Having read the diary, the Abbot's behaviour seemed far more likely. If he had killed Brother Peter, then he would have had no chance of retrieving his lost treasure. If he had left Peter with his sight then he may have eventually escaped with the treasure.

The story had finished by saying that Blind Peter spent the rest of his life working as a drudge in the Abbey. After his death, it was said that his ghost returned to look for the treasure.

Many people had claimed to have seen the ghost over the last 600 years or so. A spectral figure in a monks habit, with glowing red eyes. As an aside, Skip had also told them about the two men Blind Peter had reputedly killed to preserve his secret. The first, a man called Slone, had been exploring the tunnels below the Abbey, when he ran screaming from the maw of the tunnel and collapsed with a heart attack. The second, Mr Taylor, a builder had bought the Abbey and was planning to rip the place down. He told a friend that he had dreamed of Blind

Peter warning him away from the place. The very next day, whilst surveying the ruin a stone had fallen from the top of a crumbling arch and killed the man outright.

'Yeah, but that's just rubbish,' said Chris. 'He only told us that to stop us climbing on the walls and exploring the tunnels.' 'That worked well then.' said Tom and they both collapsed in laughter.

Tom and Chris were identical twins and thirteen years old. Now some twins live a life of telepathic intimacy, finishing each other's sentences and feeling each other's pain. Tom and Chris were not like this. Much of the time, they fought like cat and dog arguing over the smallest of things, challenging and daring each other constantly. 'I was born first,' Chris would say 'Yeah, but I'm taller Tom would reply,' and he was, but only by less than an inch. He was also slightly broader and stronger than Chris, which meant he had a slight natural advantage when it came to sports. He was, however, lackadaisical and full of whimsy, which meant that Chris could often overcome his disadvantage through determination, which he had bags of. Chris was the faster swimmer, though they were both extremely good, having qualified for the scout swimming team on three occasions. Chris's determination and single mindedness, however, did not always win him a lot of friends, people said he had a chip on his shoulder, whereas Tom's whimsy made him an instant hit with girls and boys alike. He would run up to friends screaming their name and give them a big hug, whereas Chris was more likely to sidle up and say 'Awright.'

They were both blond, but Chris was blonder, with a slight, but muscular and wiry build. Their features were best described as pinched and weasely, but not the evil weasels from toad of toad hall, more like happy smiling ferrets most of the time, especially when they were up to mischief, which they had been.

A group of them had been playing at the old ruined abbey in Netley. It had started with games of tag and 999 in, in and around the ruins. English Heritage owned the site, but it was free to enter. They did have strict rules about climbing on the walls and there were many signs posted to this effect, there was however, rarely anyone there to enforce them. The occasional tourist might frown disapprovingly in their direction, but mostly they were left to their own devices.

Which is why, having lost hide and seek, three times running, Chris decided to cheat, by climbing up onto part of the first floor which was still standing in many places. After a while he could hear that the others had all been found and had got bored looking for him, so he shouted out loudly, 'I'm over here losers.' The others came running towards his position, disappeared underneath and could be seen searching again with more enthusiasm, having climbed through the ground floor window and jumped onto the grass beyond.

He repeated the trick twice, before eventually shouting, 'Up here dummies.' This resulted in the inevitable argument about cheating, but nobody really cared. Chris showed them where he had managed to climb up and they all eventually joined him.

Casey was the first up.  He was the tallest of the group, athletic and a talented footballer.

 Tom had gone next, followed by little Chris, who struggled to reach some of the holds and had to be boosted by Luke below and pulled by Casey from above.  Luke was last up, having kept up a constant stream of concerns.  'Do you think we should be climbing on the walls, there are signs, I don't want to get in trouble, what if someone sees us, what if you fall off, what if the wall crumbles, or the ceiling falls in.  It's very old you know.'  Luke's shaggy mop of dark hair eventually crested the wall, despite his protestations and he joined the others.  'If I get in trouble I'm saying it was Chris's idea and I didn't want to be left behind.'  They all agreed that if they got in trouble, blaming Chris would be a splendid idea.  They then collapsed to the floor in a fit of giggles and broke out their lunch.

 All the stairs to the first floor had bars on them at ground level, the boys discovered, to their delight, that they did not have bars at the top.  This meant they could climb down the spiral stair cases from the top and pretend to be prisoners trapped in a cage behind the bars.

There were still parts of the walls left higher up and it looked possible to get up to a walkway, which had been part of the second floor. The conversation eventually turned to how this could be achieved and who should attempt the climb first. It was quickly agreed that Casey would go first. He was the best climber and generally agreed to be the maddest and most daring of the lot. In fact, his reputation had grown so great, that some of their parents had told them not to hang around with him. Advice, which of course, they had totally and consistently ignored. He was a laugh and what everyone needed was a laugh.

Reaching the second floor involved climbing up and around the wall, out over the edge of a drop of about twenty feet. Casey went up and then edged cautiously around over the drop. Tom had done some climbing on the wall at the local scout campsite, of course there, they had always been tied on, with a qualified instructor supervising, not nearly the same kind of buzz. He remembered the advice he had been given at the time and passed it on to Casey. 'Only move one hand or foot at a time, make sure you have three firm grips or footholds, before you move on. Test every handhold before you commit to it.' 'I know that,' shouted back Casey. This was followed by a scared sounding 'shite,' and the rattle of rocks hitting the paving slabs below. Tom had half expected the thud of a body, suddenly his confidence drained away and his knees began to shake. 'A rock pulled loose,' called Casey, his voice having returned to normal. 'You can put your hand in the hole instead.' Casey quickly pulled himself up and disappeared over the top. Soon his head popped back into view peering over the edge with a stupid grin on his face. 'Who's next then, it's amazing up here, you can see all the way to the beach.'

Tom looked down at the rocks below and wondered why he had climbed up in the first place and how he was going to get down. There weren't just butterflies in his stomach, he thought that if he didn't step back, they would be fighting to get out.

'You look a bit green there Tom,' said Chris 'Haven't turned pussy on us have you.' 'It's stupid Chris. You fall down there and you'll crack your skull open. You know I hate you, but I wouldn't want to explain to dad, how you fell off and died.' Chris was delighted at the opportunity to show his brother up and made his best chicken impersonation. 'B Geuuur,' He crowed and stepped forward.

Chris was just as nervous as Tom, but was determined to climb. He decided not to look down, just in case his nerve went. He couldn't back out now. He looked up at Casey and then fixed his gaze on the wall in front of him, choosing his first hand and footholds. He went up the first section with relative ease, but as he began the traverse round the corner, he looked down to find a foothold and couldn't help but see the dizzying drop beneath him. Chris stopped, looked up again and took a deep breath, waiting for his knees to stop shaking. He had climbed much higher before, but then he had been on a rope. This was very different. He moved with great care, following all the advice he had heard earlier, scrutinizing every rock and crevice on the wall. As his head came level with the hole Casey had made, he saw inside something stuffed in at the back. He wasn't sure what it was and he wasn't going to stop to reach down inside, it might be something nasty, so he continued the last two feet to the top.

'I think there's something in that hole you made,' he said, once his heart beat had returned to normal. 'I'm going to have a look. Hold my legs.' Chris laid on his belly and edged his upper body out over the drop, reached towards the hole with his right hand, after finding a good hold with his left. Casey flopped on his legs crushing his knee into a rock. 'Careful you knob end, that hurt.' Chris exclaimed in a high pitched voice. Casey punched him in the buttocks. 'You wanted holding, I'm holding, get on with it.' Chris shut up. He never won arguments with Casey and was in no position to do so now. He reached into the hole, half fearing that something would bite his fingers and that was how they had found the diary.

## Chapter 3

The boys were excited about the find. Casey had initially tried to take the book from Chris, claiming it was his hole he had found it in. Chris just stuffed it inside his shirt. 'We'll have a look at it when we get down,' he said, but he secretly knew, there was no way he was giving up his find. The book looked really old and might even be worth some money. The twins knew their parents were pretty skint. They tried to make sure that the twins had everything they needed, but luxuries were often in short supply. They lived above the post office and both parents worked there, but business was slow and the government was always talking about closures and changes to the post office and how they needed to get better value for money, which always meant less money for them. Their dad was brilliant and always had some money making or saving scheme on the go. Recently he had refused to pay for someone to refurbish the bathroom, after half the tiles had fallen off the wall, insisting that he could do it himself and he had. He had delved into the internet, finding all the how too guides he needed and hadn't bodged the job too badly at all. Meaning that the bathroom had returned to a usable condition within six months! The backyard, in the meantime had been used as a dumping ground for all the excavations and deliveries and packaging and debris from the working, meaning that it now resembled a building site. Not that it had resembled a garden in the first place. It had 3 sheds and a garage, joined together by various tarpaulins and bits of board. Sheltered within these structures and scattered liberally about the place were their dads projects. Mostly bits for cars and boats. He had recently bought a formula 1 powerboat, claiming he would do it up and sell it on for thousands. He had actually completed the project and the boat ran beautifully. Whenever he could afford the fuel, he would launch it at the local marina and take the boys and their friends screaming across to the island. He even let the boys drive, though the controls were different from what they had learnt to drive in Sea Scouts, having a foot pedal for the throttle like in a car. He couldn't of course, bring himself to sell the boat, so it like all other boats, had become a hole in the water in which to throw money !

'I'm not getting down yet,' said Casey. 'I want to look round here first.'  Chris wanted to look through the book, but as it was so scary getting up there in the first place, he thought he had best make the most of it.  He got up and followed Casey along the walkway.

  You could see the whole of the abbey ruin spread out below them.  South and West was the main chapel in a huge cross shape, well manicured grass growing down the nave. Directly South was the cloister square.  The walls were in place, but the covered walkways had long gone.  They were stood on top of  what was left of the accommodation block with the kitchens and latrines to the eastern end.  To the north, about 200 yards was the Abbot's lodge, still two storeys, but no roof left on the first floor and no windows or doors, but plenty of holes in the walls.  Way to the south was Southampton Water, beside it, hidden amongst the trees, was Netley Castle, which had been built with stones from the Abbey after Henry VIII had dissolved the monasteries.

There was not much of the second floor left, so soon it was time to get down. Chris laid on his belly and shuffled backwards until his legs were dangling over the edge. 'I can't find a foothold,' Chris panicked. The top of the wall was smooth, where English Heritage had poured some kind of bitumen, to stop water penetrating the exposed mortar. This was bad news for Chris, as he started to slide backwards, hands spread out flat against the smooth surface desperately trying to find some purchase. Casey grabbed his arms and laid flat, bracing his foot against a stone sticking up at the edge out of Chris's reach. The stone wobbled, but held. 'Just feel around with your feet,' shouted Casey, scared that he would get pulled over too, Chris now having a death grip on his arm. It seemed like an age, but was probably only seconds before Chris had both feet wedged into good positions and was able to lower himself until both hands could get a good grip on the edge of the wall. Once over the edge, it became easier and after a couple of moves he looked back up and smirked 'I think I shit myself,' he laughed.  'You're not the only one,' replied Casey.  I think I just saved your life.  Chris was able to complete the climb with no further incident and was soon back with the others.  Casey, having learnt from Chris's experience, laid sideways on the edge of the wall and dangled one leg over the edge to find a foothold, before proceeding down with the other.  Casey of course had no problems climbing down.

 'Look what I found,' said Chris.  He pulled the book out of his shirt and showed it to the others, a proud smile beaming from his face.  It was quite small, about the size of the little red Gideon's bible they had been given at school.  The Gideon's Bible had hundreds of pages, that were about the thickness of cigarette papers.  This book was about the same thickness, but each page was much thicker, with strange looking veins running through it and a bit ragged round the edges, as if it was handmade.  It was bound together with string along one edge.

Tom took it out of his hands, there were about twenty pages and he opened it to the first one.  The writing was tiny.  He held it up close to his face and squinted.  'I don't think it's in English, but I recognise some of the words.'  Tom started reading.

' Lat no man truste on blynd
Hen that stood in heigh degree
For hym the Abbot vileynye he al ful.
In termes hadde he casse and doomes alle.'

'Let's have a look,' says Little Chris and takes the book.  Chris is smart, well the smartest of the group.  Despite being a year younger and small for his age, he had been accepted into the group, mostly because he was a babe magnet.  The girls all thought he was cute.  He goes to a posh private school in the middle of Southampton, instead of the local one that the rest of them attend.

'I think it's some kind of old English,' said Little Chris 'Like the pub.'  'What pub,' says Tom.  'Ye Olde Whyte Harte, the spellings all wrong, but it's still English.'  'So what does it say,' questions Tom.'  'I don't know,' replies

Little Chris 'but I know someone who might. We just started doing The Pardoner's Tale in English, it's by Chaucer.  It's written in old English, but Mr Harris can read it just like normal.  He says that mostly the words are similar in sound, but the spelling is different.'

'You're not taking my book into school.' insists Chris.  'I'll never see it again.  Teachers are like that, they confiscate everything.' Chris had lost his mobile phone twice.  On the second occasion his dad had to go up the school to collect it and he hadn't given it back for another week.  He had lost count of how many cans of Relentless or packs of gum he had lost, never to see again.  'Well why don't I copy out the first few lines and see if he can translate those,' responds Little Chris and they all agree that this is probably the safest plan.  If the book is valuable, the last thing they want to do is let the authorities get hold of it.  They would probably say it belongs to English Heritage and put it in a museum, despite the fact that they never found it.

'Oy.   What are you lot doing up there. Trying to kill yourselves?.'  It was the old bloke who mowed the grass. He hated kids and was always moaning about something, even when they weren't blatantly breaking the rules.

  Casey took a running jump off the back wall and dropped the twelve feet onto the grass, doing a classic drop and roll, like a paratrooper. Tom, Chris and Luke, took a bit longer to hang by their arms and drop. 'Help.' shouts Little Chris as the rest of them start to run off. 'It's too far.' He is dangling by his arms, but won't let go. 'Just drop you pussy,' shouts Casey, but the others run back. Tom stands underneath and puts Little Chris's feet on his shoulders. Chris works his hands down the wall into a sort of crouching position, but then begins to topple. Chris and Luke grab him and they all end up in a pile on the floor. After scrambling to their feet, they race off after Casey. 'Oy. I want a word with you,' shouts the old man as he comes round the corner of the ruins. 'Come back now, or I'm calling the Police. You see if I don't. I know who you are, I've seen you here before.' His voice faded off into the distance as the boys disappeared over the fence and into the woodland beyond.

'Do you think he will,' gasps Luke. 'What,' snaps Casey. 'Call the Police of course.' 'Don't be stupid, we haven't broken any laws, were allowed in there. It's public property.' 'We did climb on the walls though,' says Luke. 'and you pulled that rock loose, that would be vandalism.' 'So, whose gonna tell them Luke. Not a grass are you.' said Casey in a threatening voice. Luke shut up and they all plodded off through the woods, back to where they had hidden their bikes.

They cycled back through Netley village, the Royal Victoria Country Park and up Lovers Lane alongside the recreation ground until they came to Hamble, where Little Chris lived.

Little Chris copied out the first four sentences in his best handwriting and slipped the piece of paper into the pocket of his blazer, all ready for school the next day. Then it was time to go home.

'So what do you reckon it says?' asks Chris 'Something about Not trusting Blondie cos he's a villain and is going to doom us all, is what it looks like.' 'Yeah, but that doesn't make much sense.' Tom perked up 'Maybe it's like a prophecy about you Blondie and how you are going to doom us all.' Chris punched his brother and stuck the book under his pillow. 'Let's hope little Chris's teacher can make more sense of it. Can I have a proper look at it? You can have it back in the morning.' Chris reluctantly agreed and handed the little book over.

 Tom went back to his room and laid on his bed. He flicked through the book looking for words he recognised, trying to get a feel for what it was about. The words eschaunge and selle seemed to feature quite heavily and Tom guessed they meant exchange and sell, so maybe it was a Merchants ledger. Tom fell asleep, with the book across his chest and the light still on.

## Chapter 4

Tom woke, it was dark and a figure stood in his doorway. 'Get lost Chris, it's still dark, you can have your book back in the morning.' The figure turns towards Tom. It's not Chris. Instead of eyes, the figure has glowing red fiery orbs set inside a black hood, with a cape sweeping to the floor. 'My booook,' the creature shrieks and flies towards Tom. He curls into a defensive ball and scrabbles back against the wall. The creature slams into him and he feels a claw like frozen hand clamp itself around his arm. It pulls and the pair of them fly through the wall. Tom screams help at the top of his voice and initially fights to break loose from the creature. Chris and Tom have bedrooms in a converted attic, they are about 30ft up, he quickly stops struggling. Tom looks down, expecting to see the high street and all the shops and houses, but they are gone. All he sees is a track through a forest. His house is gone and he doesn't know where they are. 'Take me home,' he screams, hoping someone will hear him, but the moonlit forest is deserted.

'Hooooome,' screams the creature and soon they are moving, flying, fast over the forest.

Within minutes the Abbey appears looming out of the forest, but it's not the Abbey as Tom is familiar with it. It looks like the pictures of olden days he has seen on the signs. They are about 100ft up above it and suddenly Tom is falling. The creature has faded into nothing and let him drop. He screams in terror and blacks out, before he hits the ground.

Tom awakes, he is not in pain. He wiggles his hands and feet, but his arms and legs won't move. In a panic, Tom opens his eyes, thinking he may be paralysed from the fall, which is why he is not in pain. He is in a sitting position and he is strapped to a chair. He is alone, in a stone room, with a heavy wooden door. He screams for help, shouts himself hoarse, but no one comes. Eventually, after several hours he is exhausted and falls asleep again.

Tom jerks awake. Water has been thrown over him. A muscular looking man in a

leather apron is stood over him, holding a
wooden bucket. Tom's pyjamas are soaked
and dripping with water, but to his surprise,
he also appears to be wearing a white
woollen dress of some kind, but it is hazy and
indistinct, ghostly. 'You ready to talk yet.'
Tom opens his mouth to say 'Yes, yes, what
do you want to know, I'll tell you anything,
just get me out of here, I want to go home.
What actually comes out is 'Do your worst
scum, you'll get nothing from me. Your all
going to burn in hell, I've seen what you've
been doi...' At this point the man back hands
him across the face. 'Where's the chest,' he
says. Tom tries to say 'What chest,' but what
actually comes out is 'Where you'll never find
it.' The man punches him in the face.
'Where's the chest?' Tom gives up trying to
speak. His mouth is bleeding, his nose is
bleeding, blood is running down the front of
his white robe. He can feel a loose tooth in
his mouth and he thinks his nose is broken.
'The worst you can do is kill me,' replies Tom
'and then I will go to live in bliss with my lord
in heaven.' 'Oh, shit. Oh, shit. Oh shit. I don't
want to die, don't listen to me,' thinks Tom as
the man punches him again, his right eye

closes up within seconds and he can feel more blood pouring down his cheek. 'Think this is the worst I can do,' screams the man. 'I'm just getting started. He punches Tom again face body face again, Tom looses track of how many times he has been hit, by the time he passes out.

Another bucket of water hits Tom in the face. He jerks upright every muscle in his body screaming in pain, both from the battering he has received and from being in the same position for so long. There is now a heavy wooden table to his left and his left hand is pinned to it with an iron staple, driven into the wood. His palm is flat down against the table and each finger is forced painfully apart, by nails driven in between them. He tries to pull free or move his fingers, but they are completely immobile. The man is back. He is holding a hammer. 'Want to talk to me yet, your choice, I'm going to enjoy this either way,' 'I'll never speak to you. You're going to hell, you're going to burn for eternity in one of Satan's pits,' mumbled Tom against his will.

'Aaaargh,' screams Tom.  The man has brought the hammer down, with all his might against Tom's little finger.  He looks across.  It is totally mashed.  He doubts he will ever be able to use it again.  'Where's the chest?' smash, 'Where's the chest?' smash.  Tom passes out again.

Tom wakes again, more water, several buckets by the feel of it.  His hand is agony.  He looks across.  It is just a pulped mess.  Just to look at it makes him feel sick.  He looks away.  There is a metal brazier to his right.  It is filled with coals glowing red hot.  Several metal rods are sticking out.  Directly opposite, an extremely fat man is sitting facing him.  He is wearing a white robe, made of linen and silk and trimmed with fur.  He has a large golden cross embossed with rubies and emeralds hanging on a fat golden chain round his neck.  His fat bulbous swollen hands are resting on the arms of the chair, like sausages in a butchers window.  Each finger is wrapped in gold and silver rings, with gems of every persuasion.

'Oh Peter,' He says in a sweet concerned voice 'It distresses me to see you in such a state, let me help you. All you have to do is tell me where you hid my money and I can have you out of here and in the infirmary. A soft bed and clean bandages and the tender mercies of Sister Josephine to tend your wounds. Where is my chest Peter.'

Tom gave up trying to speak, but his lips moved and words came out involuntarily as before. 'It's not your money you thief, you smuggler, you murderer.' 'Oh my. Your blasphemy saddens me, because blasphemers must be punished as you know. We mark blasphemers so everyone knows that every word that passes their lips is a lie. No one will believe these lies Peter. Everyone knows I am a godly man.' He looks to Tom's torturer. 'Do it Brother Maynard, so no one will ever believe a word he says.' The torturer drags one of the metal rods out of the fire. It has a letter 'B' glowing red on the end. He slowly brings it closer and closer to Tom's forehead. The man wraps his arm around Tom's neck and presses his sweaty, stinking, bristly cheek against Tom's own, clamping his head immobile. Searing pain burns straight into his brain, he can smell burning flesh and he can hear himself screaming at the top of his lungs, his throat ragged from the exertion.

'Last chance to speak Peter. You think things are bad now, but I can still help you, just speak to me.' Tom says nothing and neither does Peter. 'You make me sad,' says the fat man. He gets up and leaves. As he passes through the door, he looks over his shoulder and says 'I'm sure Sister Mary will be more talkative,' Tom can hear his evil laughter as he walks off up the corridor.

Tom thinks it's all over, that this is the end of his torture, but he is wrong. The torturer reaches back to his brazier and lifts another metal rod. This one double pronged, with round balls on the end of each prong. The balls are glowing red. He brings it towards Tom's face. He squeezes his eyes shut, not wanting to see what is about to happen. The metal balls burn his eyelids away and boil the aqueous humour in his eyes, until they pop, the hot clear liquid running down his face. Tom does not scream out, because he has already passed out, hoping that he never awakes.

  Tom is cold, strangely, there is little pain and he realises he can see.  He is confused, he is tied in a sitting position on the floor.  He is surrounded by soot and ash.  The stone walls totally blackened.  He is sitting in the hearth of a fire.  A man is kneeling beside him.  He has mortared a neat row of bricks to the floor along the edge of the hearth and is proceeding to start on the second layer.  He does not make eye contact with Tom and he does not speak.  Tom tries to speak.  He wants to know who the man is.  He wants to know if he will let him go.  He wants to know why he is being bricked into a hearth.

 'Hello again Mary,'  It's the fat priest again.  He has entered through the small door to the room.  'I was hoping you would be a little more talkative this time.'  Tom knows he won't be able to speak, so he doesn't try.  The priest's face comes closer and the force controlling Tom spits in his face.  'Finish the job,'  he says in a casual voice. ' Just leave one brick out for now,'  I'm sure she will change her mind in a couple of days.  Tom's view gradually diminishes brick by brick. One brick sized hole is left in the level beside his face. He sees the brick layer get up and leave. He shuts the door behind him. A tear runs down Tom's face. What is going on. He fights against his bonds, struggling to release himself, in the hope that he can kick the wall down before it sets hard and make his escape. He fights against the ropes for hours, rubbing his skin raw in the process. The space is too narrow, to turn and exert and pressure against the wall. His hands and feet are bound, but also bound to each other, he is trussed like a chicken, totally unable to help himself. Eventually, he falls asleep from exhaustion.

Tom awakens, he needs to pee desperately. The fat man is back, his blubbery lips visible through the hole in the wall. He is speaking. 'Last chance Mary. I'm a patient man, but my patience has run out. Do you have anything to say to me.' He presses his ear to the hole and holds it there for 30 seconds. Finally he says 'Fill it in.' and walks away.

Everything goes dark, Tom begins to sob, his joints are screaming with agony and his wrists and ankles are burning.  He figures pissing himself is the least of his worries.  He closes his eyes and feels the hot stream flooding his groin and running down between his legs.

He opens his eyes again to see bright light flooding though the curtains.  He is in his room, he is home, he is in bed.  Shit, shit, shit.  He has pissed the bed.  His boxers and pyjamas are soaked through and there is a big wet patch on the sheet below.  He jumps out of bed, throwing the duvet to the floor, fortunately, that is still dry.  He rips the sheet off the bed.   There is a large wet patch on the mattress.  He looks at the clock beside his bed.  It's 5am.  No one will be up for at least an hour.  There is no way Chris will let him live this down, it will be all round the school in five minutes.  He has to hide the evidence. He creeps down the hallway to the bathroom, bed sheet in hand and carefully locks the door behind him.  He finds the wet patch on the sheet, thrusts it under the tap and turns it on.  Once it is thoroughly rinsed through, he rings it out and hangs it over the radiator.  Next he strips off his pyjama bottoms and boxers and repeats the process, finally, wiping himself down with a wet flannel.

He creeps back to his room clutching his wet laundry.  He considers hanging it all on the radiator, but someone will see it if they come in.  Instead, he throws all his old clothes out of the wardrobe and onto the floor and hangs everything up inside on separate hangers.  Lastly he turns to the mattress, flannel in hand he mops it down as best he can hoping to remove any smell.  He gets a can of deodorant and sprays the wet patch. He thinks he can still smell wee, but it's not too bad.  He turns the mattress over, so the wet patch is hidden and throws his duvet over the bare mattress.  Finally, breathing a sigh of relief, he pulls on a dry pair of boxers and gets ready for school.

He starts to think about the bizarre nightmare.  Obviously, he had dreamed about the story of blind Peter, but it had been so real, so detailed.  Even now, knowing it was a dream, it filled him with horror.  His muscles were aching, nothing like he had imagined in his dream, but still sore.  He picks Chris's book up off the floor, wondering if it had anything to do with his nightmare, vowing to return it to Chris at the earliest opportunity.

  Tom leaves the book on his bedside table and goes downstairs to the kitchen.  'Blimey, wonders will never cease, what happened, shit the bed?'  It was dad, he was always up early and irritatingly cheerful for such an obscene hour.  He normally had to wake the boys at least twice before they would get up on a school day.  Tom grunted 'No,' his cheeks going red at the thought of the wet stuff hanging in the wardrobe, but dad didn't notice. He had his back to Tom filling the kettle.  'Fancy a cuppa.' he said.  'Nah.  I only want cereals.' replied Tom.

  Tom had finished breakfast and Dad had disappeared downstairs to the Post Office, when Chris arrived in the kitchen clutching his book.  Tom looked at it nervously, but didn't say anything about his nightmare. Instead he said 'Don't go waving that around, hide it in your room.'  Chris shrugged and turned to go back upstairs.  'and stay out of my room, you know I hate it when you go in there without me.  I was going to give you the stupid book.'

# Chapter 5

It was half way through Maths when Chris felt his pocket vibrating.  It was algebra and dead boring.   Mr Yates was the worst teacher in the school.  He spoke in a dreary bored monotone, always made you work from the book and couldn't control the class at all.  He didn't teach he lectured and expected you to copy everything he wrote on the board.  Which was important, because half the time you couldn't hear what he was saying because of the noise in the class.  He would hand out the occasional detention if you hadn't written anything in your book and he happened to notice, but mostly he would just set a task from the book and retreat behind his desk, vainly hoping that they might complete it.  They were supposed to be simplifying algebraic expressions, but Chris didn't have a clue what he was doing, so was just copying the questions, ready to fill in the answers when Mr Yates read them out at the end of the lesson.  That way he had successfully avoided detention for months.

Chris slid his phone into his lap and glanced down at the screen. It was a text message from Little Chris.

Mr Harris says its Middle English
Don't trust important people blindly. The Abbot is a vile criminal.
He has given me a dictionary of middle English, but also showed me how I can download it online.

Chris texted back. Brilliant. Come round mine later. He couldn't wait for Maths to finish. Nothing new there, but it was break time next and he had a cunning plan.

The bell finally went and Chris was out the door before Mr Yates even had time to say in his nasal drone 'The bell is for me not for you.'

He charged up the stairs to the reprographics room and put on his most ingratiating smile. He knocked on the door and went in. 'Hello Miss, I have to photocopy this little book to use in my art project.' The reprographics lady barely looked at his book and just nodded towards the old machine in the corner that she let the students use. 'Don't be too long, I'm on me break.' Chris carefully copied each page and enlarged it so it was easier to read. It also meant there would be space to write on the sheets. He carefully numbered and folded each sheet and placed them in his bag with the book.

Then he texted Casey and Luke and told them all to meet round his house after school, 5pm would allow Little Chris time to get back from Southampton.

Once they had all arrived Little Chris showed them the middle English dictionary. They then downloaded it onto their various smart phones and Ipads. He spread out the first sheet on the floor. Many of the words are obvious he says, so don't worry about them, just look for the really weird ones or anything that doesn't make sense. He demonstrated with the first few sentences, scribbling words underneath the text. It doesn't always read in order, they used quite a lot of French at the time the grammar can be quite weird.

Lat no man truste blyndee
Let no man trust blindly

Hem that stood in heigh degree.
Those that stand in high office.

For hym the Abbot vileynye he al ful
For he the Abbot is full of vileness

In termes hadde he casse and doomes all
He knows all convictions common and
criminal

Chris shares out the photocopied sheets
between his friends and they set to work
spreading their papers out across the floor.
Chris had never worked so hard.  Much of it is
still nonsense, but a theme was starting to
become clear.  It is largely a list of crimes
committed by the Abbot, with times dates,
lists of goods, monies or people involved,
with occasional comments by the author.
Eventually it was time to go home.  Chris
asked everyone to finish translating their
pages by Friday.  Not everyone was keen on
the idea.  'What's the point,' said Casey 'It's
rubbish, just give it to Little Chris's teacher,

he'd probably enjoy translating it.' 'We could do that,' says Tom, 'but aren't you beginning to wonder what happened to all this money the Abbot stole.' Tom thought about sharing his nightmare with the group, but instead just said 'What if some of it's still around down there. There might be a clue in this book!' 'Like I said,' said Casey. 'Everyone better have their bit complete by Friday.'

'Chris. I think I know who wrote this diary,' said Tom. 'Who,' queried Chris. 'It's blind Peter, the monk from the story. I think he was real. I saw him in a dream last night. More of a nightmare really.' Tom gives Chris a summary of, last nights, nightmare. The apparition, the flight, the fall, the torture, the broken hand, the branding, his eyes and finally being walled up. He left out the last bit, but emphasised how real it had felt, how scared he was, how genuinely painful it had felt and how he was aching the next morning. 'Do you think it's the ghost of Blind Peter trying to scare us off like Slone and that builder' said Chris. 'It was more like I was experiencing his life,' said Tom, 'but I know I don't want that book anywhere near me tonight.'

 The next few days passed without incident until Chris gets an excited phone call from Casey. 'I know where it is,' he gushes, 'the treasure, the Abbots booty, Blind Peter buried it in the tunnels.' 'Does it say where?' asks Chris, 'Those tunnels are proper long.' 'I haven't found anything about that yet,' says Casey 'but he outlines a plan to drop a chest of gold down the Abbots bog and then drag it along the tunnels to a place where he has hollowed out the wall. One of the others might have found more details. We have to get down there and have a look.' 'I will try and find some plans for the Abbey online,' says Chris, 'It might give us some clues where to look. If nothing else we will be able to see how long the tunnel is.' They say their goodbyes and hang up. Chris passes the news onto Tom and they Google Netley Abbey.

 The boys spend the next hour going through every page they can find about the Abbey. There are many pages describing the history of the Abbey, when it was built, when it was dissolved, how it was turned into a manor house.  There are many photos of the current ruin and the odd painting of what it would have looked like back in medieval times.  They even read through a detailed description of all the rooms and what they would have been used for.  Not one of the sites mentions the tunnels that run beneath the ruin, despite the fact that they are an unmissable part of the ruins for anyone who has explored the site.  Tom had even climbed down into the drainage channel, where it passed through the kitchen, after losing a football over the wooden railing that protects visitors from falling in.  There was a considerable amount of rubbish in it.  Obviously the old gardener was unable to climb down to clear it.

  'How come the tunnels don't even get a mention on a single website' queries Chris.  'It's not possible in this day and age to keep something like that secret.  It would mean that no one has written about or photographed the tunnels for hundreds of years.  Why would they ignore a feature as amazing as that?' 'Maybe the ghost stopped them' says Tom. 'It's been protecting it's treasure all this time. It's stopped builders, poets, authors, architects, surveyors, painters and even English Heritage from mentioning the tunnels, because that's where the treasure is still buried.' states Tom in an excited and triumphant tone. 'How would it do that,' says Chris. 'Visiting them in dreams, like it did me. Killing them like that builder. Maybe we should stay away.' replies Tom. 'Not a chance.' States Chris, 'This is our chance to be rich. Monks are supposed to help the poor, and that's us.' 'Really? We're not that poor Chris. Just cos we weren't allowed on the school ski trip, doesn't make us poor.' insists Tom. 'Ok, Well I don't mind donating some to charity, the Sea Scouts could do with some new boats and a refurbished HQ for starters,' acquiesces Chris. 'That should get us on his good side. How much do you think a chest of medieval gold coins would be worth?' They both scramble for the computer again and Google gold coins.

The oldest gold coin they can find on ebay is from 1509 and so far the auction had reached £12,000 for one coin! 'If there are a thousand coins in this chest,' babbles Chris, 'That would be twelve million pounds! Have you got a torch, we have to have a look in those tunnels.' 'Have you forgotten what happened to that guy Slone when he went into the tunnels looking for the treasure. He ran out screaming block them up, block them up and dropped dead of a heart attack.' warns Tom. 'And what about that nightmare I had. It's already warning us away. I think we should forget it,' 'Stop being a pussy Tom. It was only a nightmare. This is twelve million we're talking about here.' argues Chris. 'Is it worth dying for?' asks Tom, which seems to end the argument.

The next day Tom and Chris meet up with Casey and Luke at school. They disappear to the far end of the playing fields against the fence, where it's hidden by large bushes. Fortunately there are no smokers hiding there, so they make their plans. Despite Tom's protestations, they all agree to get permission to camp out in Luke's back garden on Saturday night. He lives the closest to the Abbey. They will bring torches, backpacks and tools for digging. They will go to bed early, but sleep with their clothes on and set the alarm for midnight. Luke's parents are usually in bed by 10:00 and Luke's little sister goes way before that. That should give them at least 6 hours to get to the Abbey, find the treasure and get back to Luke's house.

## Chapter 6

The tent is small and green, with clear
Perspex panelled windows in the front and a
door with two zips.  It's an old ridge tent, not
one of the cool new dome ones.  It's about 20
years old and had belonged to Luke's dad.
It's a four man tent and tents are never
generous with the amount of space they give
a man.  The porch is jammed with bags and
the boys are stuffed in the inner, not like
sardines, more like a dog pile, arms legs and
heads every which way, some in and some
out of their multicoloured sleeping bags.
  Beep, beep, beep.  Someone's phone goes
off.  Then another playing one of the latest
tunes.  There is a general groaning about
getting up, but then they remember what
they are about to do and a wave of
adrenaline hits them.  The phones are
silenced, eyes are rubbed, limbs are
stretched and eventually the door zips slowly
creep upwards.  Luke's tousled head pokes
out and he looks up at his house.  It's a
modern red brick semi-detached with a path
running down one side to a gate into the

back garden.  More importantly, the lights are all out.

 'Okay let's go.' Whispers Luke.  'No talking until we get away from here and don't bang the gate.'  Luke knows that if they get caught sneaking out at night he will be grounded for a month.  The boys file out in silence, collecting their bags and pulling on jackets. They slowly disentangle their bikes from the pile on the floor and one by one creep out the side gate, pushing their bikes.

  They cycle across the road and past the mounds known locally as 'Telly-tubby hills'. Really, the mounds are buried air raid shelters.  The whole estate is built on a former WWII airfield.  All the old buildings and hangers had been demolished to build houses, but the bunkers were too tough, so had just been buried in the middle of the estate.  Luke leads them towards a cut way at the back of his house that leads down a footpath, well away from any traffic.  They come out not far from Lovers lane, but have to cross the main road into the village.  Now most villages would be quiet by midnight, but not Hamble.  It is a party village and has the best social life outside of Southampton.

There are over twenty licensed bars, restaurants, takeaways, social clubs and Yacht Clubs, many of them still busy at midnight, so there are still cars and Taxis regularly passing the crossing point.  Luke waves the others to stop, well back from the road.  The Police are regular visitors to Hamble and they would definitely stop to see what five young boys were doing out at this time of night on bikes with no lights.

  Eventually, all is quiet and Luke waves them across.  They start cycling down Lovers Lane, but once under the trees and away from the street lights it is pitch black.   They gradually get slower and slower until Luke stops and they all run into each other.  Little Chris tumbles off into a holly bush to his right and curses loudly.  'What the **** did you stop for. **** I've got holly stuck right up my ****.'  'I can't see ****, numb nuts, what do you expect me to do,' shouts back Luke.' 'Shut-up. I've cycled down here before in the dark.' says Casey.  'All you have to do is look upward.  The trees meet in the middle above the path and there is a slightly lighter patch you can follow.'  'Or we can get the torches out.' Says Chris. 'There'll be no one around down here to see us. I am not riding into a holly bush in the dark.' They all agree to break out the torches and continue down the muddy track without further incident.

At the bottom of the track they turn left onto graveyard road. To the right, the road runs down to the old military graveyard. 'Glad were not going any nearer the graveyard,' says Little Chris timidly 'It is well spooky out here.' The graveyard road is on a raised embankment that runs across a wooded valley. The embankment is 30ft high in places with steep muddy slopes running down either side. The slopes are seriously eroded in places and are starting to undermine the roadway. In the valley below there is mist between the trees. Anything could be hiding down there. 'Stay in the middle,' calls Casey. He has been leading since the collision. Tom has been at the back all the way and has said nothing. The thought of visiting the Abbey again fills him with dread. It is all he can do to keep following the others.

Casey leads on through the Royal Victoria Country Park.  They have often played wide games down here at night with the sea scouts, so the layout is comforting, even in the dark and they start to feel more confident.  It is also lighter.  The park has wide open fields, roads and car parks, so they are no longer under the tree cover.

They quickly reach the park gates, which are always open, there are houses in the park and the residents need access twenty four seven.

Casey stops the group.  They are about to enter Netley Abbey village.  'What do we say if anyone asks us where were going?' he questions.  'There won't be anyone around at this time,' says Chris.  'If we do come across anyone, ignore them and keep going.  If it's the cops or someone tries to follow us by car, there is a footpath off new road we can disappear up.'  They all agree to the plan and follow Chris.  They pass through the village without incident and reach St Edwards church.  St Edwards is a small stone built church with a tower and has a prefabricated church hall standing incongruously beside it.

It has houses either side of it, but behind is woodland, which backs onto the Abbey. They cycle round the back and hide their bikes in the woods. This is their normal route into the Abbey, especially when the gate at the front is closed to visitors, which it often is. There is a house beside the gate, where a warden is supposed to live, but there is rarely anyone at home. The back route is still the safest route, for a kid who may have to make a fast exit.

  They weave their way down through the woods to the hole in the fence at the bottom and slide one at a time underneath it. 'Torches off,' orders Chris. 'If the wardens awake, we don't want him seeing light and calling the cops. We'll go in round the back, that way we stay further from his house.' They all turn off their torches and follow Chris in a crouching run across the lawn to the back wall of the abbey. They climb in through a window into what they think used to be the infirmary or Latrines. From the plans they had found, it looked like the infirmary had been on the ground floor, with the Latrines on the floor above, besides the monks dormitories. Either way, the floor above is mostly gone and the tunnel is exposed as it runs through the edge of this room, with only a wooden railing to separate the gravel floor of the infirmary from the twenty foot drop into the rubbish strewn drainage channel. 'Only one torch,' state's Chris. 'Mine. I'm gonna keep it pointed downward, so it's less noticeable from outside.' They all stand nervously at the railing and look over the side at the rubbish illuminated in the torch beam below. Chris sweeps the torch from side to side. To the right, the channel passes under an archway into the kitchen, to the left it disappears into a tunnel, which they can't see up from this angle.

'Who's going first?' asks Chris nervously. 'You.' replies Casey. 'I would,' says Chris, 'but I'm holding the torch.' 'So, me as usual then,' says Casey in a heroic tone. 'You are the best climber,' ingratiates Chris.

Casey steps over the railing onto the ledge the other side. He leans across the channel and places his right hand against the far wall, then reaches across with his right foot and plants it lower down against an outcropping rock. Then with a hand and foot braced on either side he gradually climbs down. As he gets lower the rocks become mossy and damp. The floor of the tunnel wet and slimy as he touches down. He looks up to the others, their anxious faces looking over the railing. 'Who's next then,' he whispers. Chris follows. Carefully placing his feet in the same places Casey used. The climb is easy. Luke and even Little Chris quickly follow. Tom hesitates at the top. 'I think one of us should stay here.' he says. 'In case anything goes wrong. I could go for help.' The others look up at him dubiously. 'It's just common sense.' he states more confidently. 'Anything could happen, what if the tunnel collapses.' 'You sure you're not just wimping out on us Tom,' queries Casey. 'Do you want to know that help is on the way if you get stuck down there.' responds Tom. 'Head up towards the Abbot's Lodge, I will go above ground and meet you at the other end. Does anyone have a signal on their phone?' They all did, but only one bar. Casey turns on his torch and heads into the end of the tunnel holding his phone in his other hand. After thirty seconds he is back. 'You go a few yards into the tunnel and the signal goes completely.' he says, confirming their suspicions. 'We need a plan, so I know when to start panicking.' says Tom, with a nervous laugh. 'We'll head straight up towards the Abbot's Lodge and meet you at the other end.' states Chris. 'If we aim to be there within half an hour and back here within the hour if we can't get through. It's one thirty now, so if we're not back by two thirty start panicking.' 'If you're not back by two thirty I call the Police.' Says Tom nervously. Realising that he has just volunteered to spend up to an hour on his own in what he knows to be a haunted ruin. 'Can someone else stay with me?' he asks. 'No,' responds Casey, 'no one else is staying, we've wasted enough time already. Let's go.'

No one dares to argue and as he heads into the mouth of the tunnel they turn and follow, switching on torches as they go. The tunnel is three feet wide and about five foot high, with an arched roof. It is constructed completely of stone, floor and ceiling, but in places, the odd stone has fallen out of the wall or roof.  The first missing rock they come to, Luke drops his backpack to the floor, pulls out a garden trowel and starts to dig around in the hole.  Dirt cascades out and forms a damp pile on the floor of the tunnel.  'Easy psycho,' screeches Little Chris, 'are you trying to bury us alive.'  'This is what we're here for,' argues Luke.  'We won't find anything if we don't look properly.'  'Hold it.' commands Casey.  He also drops his backpack and pulls out the biggest sheath knife the boys have ever seen.  The blade is at least six inches long.  He proceeds to jam it up to its hilt in the loose earth in the hole.  'No hidden chests in there,' he states.  '**** is that even legal?' asks an astonished Little Chris.  'Not even close,' replies Casey  'so don't go blabbing.'  He tests the next few holes in the same way, until he comes to a hole in the roof. 'Leave it,' says Little Chris  'You'll bring the roof down, besides, you couldn't lift a chest up there.'  They carefully skip past the hole in the roof, doing their best to carefully skirt the area directly underneath the missing stone.  The tunnel floor gradually gets wetter and they have to skirt the odd small puddle. The puddles get bigger until eventually they reach one that covers the floor side to side. It stretches for about six foot. Casey, who is still leading, stops briefly, steps back and takes a running jump and comfortably clears the water. Luke who is following repeats the feat, but Little Chris lands short by about a foot, making a large splash. '****, these are my best trainers.' Squawks Little Chris. Luke looks smugly down at his hiking boots and waterproof trousers. Chris crosses without incident and they continue on.

  Within five minutes Tom is starting to get anxious. He has been standing by the wooden railing, watching the glow from the torches quickly fade and then straining his ears to hear the slightest noise from the tunnel, but eventually these fade as well. He is about to leave, when he hears a sound. It's a flapping noise, like laundry in the wind, he imagines a robe might sound similar if someone were running in one. There are four exits from the infirmary. East is the wooden railings and the tunnels. He has no intention of following the others down there. South is a doorway leading into the kitchen next door, west is a doorway leading through the chapter house alongside the cloisters. The noise he heard came from this direction, so he retreats to the north towards the window through which he entered. The ground is covered in a fine grey gravel. Tom treads as carefully as he can ensuring he does not scatter the loose gravel and give his position away. It takes him a whole minute to creep the ten yards to the window. He climbs up onto the window sill and crouches there ready to jump, straining to hear a repeat of the noise. His heart is beating like a drum and it seems so loud that if someone is creeping up on him, then they must surely hear it. Then he hears the noise again, closer. Followed by the cooing of a pigeon. Relief floods him and his hammering heart gradually slows.

Tom decides to make his way across to the Abbot's Lodge and wait there. There is a wider field of view and if there is anyone or thing around then he will be more likely to see them coming.

He jumps out of the window and begins walking across the damp lawn that separates the infirmary from the Abbot's Lodge.  If they can walk up the tunnel as fast as he can walk across the lawn, then they may only be a couple of minutes he thinks.  He scans the Lodge ahead of him, searching for any signs of movement, when out of the corner of his eye he catches a glimpse of movement, a figure entering the chapel to his left.  He is exposed in the centre of the lawn, so he sprint across to the wall of the Chapter house and peers through the window, in time to see the figure quickly gliding across the cloister square.  He ducks down and in a crouch he runs across to the infirmary door.  Where he stops frozen.  The figure is floating up over the wooden railing above the tunnel.  It turns and looks directly at him it's glowing red eyes aflame with anger.  'I tried to warn you.'  It screeches.  'Now another must die.  No one will touch the treasure until my Mary lies at peace.'

## Chapter 7

'No please stop.  Don't kill anyone.  I tried to stop them, they wouldn't listen.'  Screams Tom tears pouring down his face, but it is too late.  The ghost disappears below the railing without another sound.  Tom sprints to the side, leans over the edge and shouts as loud as he can.  'Get out of there.  Blind Peter is coming.  He is going to kill you.'

  The tunnel has collapsed.  Not the roof, but the floor and part of the walls.  A gaping hole is in the floor and some of the wall has fallen into it.  The hole has filled with water and it looks dark and deep.  'Well, that looks like it,' says Little Chris.  'We can't get any further.'  'I think I could jump it,'  says Casey.  'Yeah, but what about the rest of us.'  says Little Chris.  'Wait here.  We can get you on the way back.'  Casey backs up a few steps further than last time and again, comfortably makes the leap.  Luke goes next and although he lands in the water has still jumped far enough to hit solid paving stones beneath.   Little Chris is still debating whether to attempt the jump, when they hear a load scream from behind.  The

Chris's turn in unison to see two blazing eyes surging toward them. 'Move it,' shouts Chris and pushes his smaller namesake towards the expanse of water. Little Chris, totally unprepared, makes a feeble leap and falls well short. His best trainers disappear below the water, quickly followed by his beige Chinos, his blue Hollister hoodie and finally his panic stricken face. His short brown hair disappears below the inky black water, but immediately bobs back up as Little Chris splashes and thrashes towards the edge of the drop where Luke and Casey are reaching out to pull him in. 'Get out of the way.' screams Chris. He looks round to check on the progress of the fiend, but it's too late. It's upon him, arms thrust forward reaching for his neck. He stumbles backward away from its grasp, one foot hits nothing but water and he topples backwards.

 Two black claw like hands sink into his neck. Their touch like ice. Those burning eyes thrust forward until all he can see is fire engulfing him. He screams in agony as the fire hits his eyes and burns inwards, deep into his skull. Blinded, he hits the water, still screaming and swallows a huge mouthful. In his panic he sucks in another lungful of water before finally passing out from pain and lack of oxygen.

Casey and Luke drag Little Chris clear of the water and shine their torches, hurriedly, back across the expanse.  The ghost has gone. Chris bobs to the surface, but he is floating face down, the air trapped in his coat, forming a bubble that holds it up.  Casey drops his torch and knife, scrambles out of his backpack and leaps into the water, virtually landing on Chris, but getting him in a firm grasp.  He flips him over in the water and drags him back towards the others.  They drag him out onto the flagstones, his body limp and unresponsive, water running from his mouth and nose.  Suddenly, he coughs and vomits a jet of water onto the floor.  He coughs again and again until gradually the coughing subsides.  He lifts himself onto his hands and knees, sits back on his heels and raises his head.  His eyes are squeezed tight shut, but in the torchlight, the boys can see a red glow emanating from within.  His eyes flick open to reveal fire, his mouth opens and flames spew forth, followed by an unholy scream that deafens the boys with its intensity.

Casey, Luke and Little Chris plunge back into the water and scramble across, trying to distance themselves from the monster Chris has become. 'Get out, get out, get out, you are unworthy.' screams Chris as he turns to follow. They charge back down the tunnel, only one torch left between them, clutched vicelike in Luke's hand, its beam bouncing randomly, casting shadows up and down the tunnel ahead. Behind them they hear the splash of the monster as it passes through the water and then a roaring battle cry as it charges after them.

They burst out of the tunnel and all three begin to simultaneously shimmy up the wall, knowing that Chris, or the thing that Chris has become is too close behind them, knowing that whoever is slowest will be caught, that maybe all of them will be dragged back down before they can reach the top. Tom is there above them urging them on. He has stepped over the railing and is stood on the ledge the other side, reaching down ready to help. In his urgency to scramble up the wall, Little Chris slips, his right foot in its sodden slippery trainer sliding from the rock. He tumbles back to the rubbish strewn floor below. As he scrambles desperately back to his feet Chris bursts from the maw of the tunnel flame pouring from every orifice. Little Chris screams as the monster quickly closes on him. 'Help me, Heeeeelp.' His cries are cut off as the monsters hands close around his neck.

Without warning, the monster collapses, like a marionette, with its strings cut. It drops to the floor. The fire has gone out and it is just Chris again. Little Chris slumps to the floor beside him. His legs have turned to jelly and can no longer hold him. 'What's wrong with Chris.' shouts Tom as he starts to climb rapidly down towards him, jumping the last six feet in his urgency to reach his stricken sibling, 'The ghost got him,' sobs Little Chris as he gasps for breath. Tom kneels beside his brother and shakes him. Shouting his name, 'Chris, Chris, wake up its Tom, can you hear me,' Tom leans his face down and puts his cheek to the body's mouth. 'He's still breathing.' He announces. Chris groans and opens his eyes. This time, they are his eyes, real and undamaged. He looks up into Toms concerned face and smiles. 'What happened,' he groans.

Despite his ordeal, Chris is quickly back on his feet and manages the climb back out unaided. Tom and Little Chris follow and they all gather at the top. 'Oh my god,' says Little Chris, 'I thought we were all going to die. I am never going back in those tunnels again, my hands are still shaking.' He holds his hand out for all to see. It is clearly trembling. 'I think you shit yourself too,' laughs Casey, pointing at a large muddy streak down Little Chris's trousers. They all start to laugh, more from the relief of their narrow escape, than from Casey's poor joke.

'Let's get back,' says Luke. 'I'm soaked, I want to go home, I can't bear it here another minute.' 'What are we going to tell our parents?' asks Tom. 'Your all dripping wet.' 'We'll worry about that later,' replies Casey 'Let's get out of here.' They all quickly follow him through the infirmary window and run across the grass.  They don't stop running until they get to their bikes, by then they are gasping for air and Little Chris has fallen behind.  They scramble onto their bikes and wait for Little Chris before pedalling for home.

They are halfway across the park, when Little Chris shouts for them to stop.  Once they have all cruised to a halt, he pauses a moment to catch his breath and says.  'I can't go home like this, all covered in mud, my mum will kill me and she will want to know what we have been up to.'  'What do you suggest?' asks Tom.  'Netley Sailing Club is just down here and I have my members key, I always keep it with my house key.  It'll get us into the changing rooms, even when the club is closed, we can at least wash off in warm showers.'  'Yeah, says Luke 'and we have a tumble drier in the garage, no one will hear it from the house, we can get everything dry before my parents get up.   They're never up early on a Sunday anyway.'

They cycle down the hill to the sailing club. At two in the morning it is quiet and dark.

Little Chris turns the key in the lock and they all bundle in behind him.  The automatic lights turn on, but there is no danger of anyone investigating, the club is isolated on the shoreline at the edge of the park and hidden behind a row of bushes.  They turn the water on and the electric showers quickly run hot.  The four cold wet boys step under the hot stream and allow the warm water to soak into their clothes.  Tom sits well to one side, knowing that eventually someone will try to splash him.

  'What happened to you Chris?' asks his brother 'your eyes were on fire.'  'I don't know,' replies Chris  'The ghost got me.  His eyes were on fire and then they burnt into my head.  It was agony.  I thought I was dead and then everything went black.  Next thing I know, your kneeling beside me.'  'How come your all wet?' Tom proceeds 'There's a big hole full of water across the tunnel.' replies Little Chris, busily trying to rub the muddy stain out of his best chinos.  'We were in a bit of a hurry to cross when the ghost chased us.'

The boys begin to warm up.  Little Chris pulls off a trainer and fills it with water. 'Leave it out Chris,' says Tom.  'What, I'm only washing the mud out.' replies Little Chris and hurls the contents of his shoe half heartedly towards Tom.  'Don't you think we have enough stuff to get dry,' responds Tom angrily, despite the fact that the water had missed him by a mile.  He knew he had to discourage the others, otherwise a full blown water fight would have developed, with him as the only victim.  The others reluctantly agreed that now was not the time and after washing the mud out of their shoes they put them back on and squelch towards the exit.

It was a cold fast cycle sprint back to Luke's house.  The boys aware that the brisk exercise will help to keep them warm.  They arrive at Luke's side gate and creep back through with their bikes, carefully laying them on the floor.  Luke opens the back door to the garage and they all stream inside. 'Tom,' says Luke  'I need you to sneak up to the bathroom and get four towels out of the cupboard.  If anyone wakes up, just tell them you needed the loo.  Oh, and leave your shoes by the back door, they're muddy.' Tom heads off and the boys begin to strip, each creating a wet pile of clothes on the floor beside them, Luke throwing his, including his boots, directly into the tumble drier. By the time Tom returns, they are all stood in their boxers waiting. They dry themselves, wrap the towel round their waists and discard their underwear. Luke turns the drier on and sets it on maximum heat for two hours. It should be dry in an hour he says and we can put the next lot in. They shuffle back to the tent, ditch their towels and snuggle down into their sleeping bags. Tom sets an alarm for one hour on his phone. The others then realise that their phones are still in their pockets and Luke has to rush back out to retrieve his from the tumble drier before it is completely destroyed. They all discuss the best ways to dry mobile phones and agree that taking it apart, removing the battery and SIM card and then leaving it in the airing cupboard to thoroughly dry before putting it back together is their best chance.

 They do not sleep, they can't, there is too much to say and too much adrenaline still flowing through their veins. Each hour, one

more of them departs, returning wearing dry
boxers and carrying a bundle of clothing,
which they dump in the porch of the tent. By
six in the morning the tumble drier eventually
gets a rest. The birds have been singing for
an hour and the sky is light, but finally the
five boys drop into a deep and dreamless
sleep.

## Chapter 8

'Come on you lot, wakey wakey!' calls Luke's Dad. 'It's nearly lunchtime. The days a wasting. At your age I was out having adventures by now.' The boys did eventually surface and spent the afternoon chilling in Luke's room, playing computer games and chatting about the nights events, when no parents or nosey sisters were in earshot. They all agreed to give up on the idea of treasure hunting and thought that handing the diary over to English Heritage was the most honest way to dispose of it. Chris agreed to push it through the letter box of the wardens house at the Abbey with a note, saying where it had been found. Eventually it was time to go.

It is dinner time. Chris and Tom are sat in front of the television with their food on their laps, a roast dinner that their mum had spent the afternoon cooking. "How was the sleepover then?' asks their dad. 'You haven't said a thing since you got in. Did you get much sleep?' 'Nah, the usual,' replies Tom 'We spent all night talking and all morning sleeping and then mucked about on Luke's computer.' 'Are you okay Chris?' asks dad 'You look really pale, have you been crying, your eyes look slight bloodshot.' 'No. I'm fine.' responds Chris grumpily. 'He probably got poked in the eye, when we were fighting last night.' fills in Tom, looking at Chris' eyes curiously. They waste the evening watching television, despite the fact that they have homework due in tomorrow. They have already told mum they didn't have any, so couldn't very well get it out now. Eventually, they traipse upstairs to their bedrooms in the attic.

Tom awakes. There is a heavy weight on his bed and someone is shaking him. He opens his eyes to see Chris sitting ramrod straight on the edge of his bed, wearing nothing but his boxers. It was a warm evening and the boys commonly slept this way. His feet are on the floor and his knees together, like a very prim old fashioned school mistress. He is facing away from Tom, but has reached across with his right arm and is still shaking him. 'Alright, I'm awake,' moans Tom 'what the hell do you want.' 'We must help Mary,'

intones Chris, his voice dull and lifeless.
'Mary, Mary who?' questions Tom. 'Sister
Mary, we must help her.' continues Chris.
'How?' asks Tom 'It's the middle of the
night.' 'We must go to her.' Chris turns his
face to meet Tom's. His eyes are once again
alight with fire. Tom shoves his duvet aside
and scrambles backwards up towards the top
of his bed, filling his lungs ready to scream,
but he is too late. Chris reaches out and
grasps him by the shoulder. At Chris's touch
the room fades around the pair and Tom
finds himself once again floating above a dark
forest, accompanied by his brother.

They fly to the Abbey, but this time Tom is
not dropped and does not find himself tied to
a chair being tortured. Instead, they fly
towards the Abbot's Lodge and through the
wall, they are as insubstantial as ghosts. The
Lodge is new and shiny, with a heavy wooden
door and clean wooden shutters at the
windows. The interior is opulent. Tom looks
towards his brother. Chris is still possessed
by the ghost, his eyes still afire. Through
Chris's frame, Tom can see two figures,
struggling with a heavy wooden chest. It is he

assumes Brother Peter and Sister Mary. They carry it across the room, by black iron handles attached at either end. Chris and Tom float across the room towards the pair and follow them out the back door of the lodge, into a small latrine. Peter lifts the wooden cover clear, to reveal a deep and smelly hole.

They have a rope, which they attach to the handles of the chest and then lift it to the edge of the hole. 'Brace yourself,' says Peter as he leans back against the rope taking the strain and simultaneously kicks the chest into the hole. They are both jerked forward by the weight, but manage to hold it and gradually lower the heavy chest to the floor of the tunnel below. Once the strain is relieved Peter coils the rope and drops it into the hole as well. He turns towards Mary, takes her in his arms and hugs her. He then plants a tender kiss on her forehead and strokes her cheek. 'Go about your duties as normal,' he says 'I will hide the chest until suspicions have been allayed and then we can distribute the Abbots ill gotten wealth.' Peter leaves the Abbot's Lodge. It is late afternoon and the sun is just peaking above the treetops casting shadows across the monastery grounds.  He does not notice a shadowy figure watching him leave the shelter of the doorway.  As he crosses to the chapter house, the hooded figure detaches itself from the shadows and follows Peter.  A few minutes later Sister Mary leaves the Abbot's Lodge and heads towards the kitchens and warming rooms.  Chris and Tom follow her involuntarily drifting across what would have been lawns in their day, but are currently kitchen gardens, criss-crossed with tiny paths, which allow them to be tended. She hurries into the kitchens and after a brief exchange with another nun working there, she collects a large pot of what looks like stew and struggling slightly under its weight she takes it through to the refectory where many monks, lay brothers, nuns, visitors and village workmen are waiting.  She places the large pot on the end table and begins dolling the stew into small wooden bowls.  A monk arrives with a cloth covered tray and begins dishing out small loaves to the assembled masses.  The room is quiet, with wooden tables and benches, but a fire is burning in the end wall, the same one that the kitchen staff have been using from the other side and the atmosphere is warm and friendly.

When the meal is complete, the diners collect their bowls and wooden spoons and return them to Mary's table. There is not a scrap of stew left in any of the bowls and they have been wiped clean with chunks of bread. She piles them all into the now empty pot and carts them through to the kitchens where she proceeds to wash and clean and wipe, with hot water from a pot above the fire.
Eventually, her tasks complete, she leaves and heads for the south wing of the monastery, where she disappears inside, followed by other nuns.

Time seems to speed up for Chris and Tom as they float outside the Nun's quarters. The moon appears in the sky, but it tracks across at amazing speed and within moments, the sun is once again peaking over the treetops. 'Why are we here?' asks Tom looking towards his brother. 'What do you want us to do?' 'Watch,' is Chris's one word reply.

Tom watches as Mary collects water in a bucket and returns to the nun's quarters. Minutes later she is hurrying back towards the kitchens.  She collects a barrow load of wood along the way and once inside she begins to coax the fire back into life.  She helps prepare a thin grey unappetizing mixture of mashed grain, milk and water, which she warms on the fire, before distributing to the waiting masses.  She finishes her duties in the kitchen and heads across to the Abbot's Lodge, where she is met by a burly looking monk.  He is in his thirties, has a scar running down his right cheek and is not clean shaven, or particularly clean looking.  'The Abbot is expected back at noon,' he says,  'Make sure the fires are well stoked and his apartments warm by the time he arrives or there'll be the devil to pay.'  Mary busies herself for about an hour, carting logs, re-filling the log piles beside the fire places and laying fires in all the hearths.  She also leaves an earring on the floor in a store off the Abbots bedroom.   Eventually, she lights the fires and once they are burning strongly she adds more wood and departs.  It appears she is not on lunch duty as she enters the refectory and collects bread, cheese and an apple from baskets on the end table. Brother Peter is in sat eating alone. She glances at him, but goes to sit with some other nuns, who are clustered together talking.

 The talk is about the Abbots imminent return. 'Are his fires roaring Mary?' says one of the other sisters, 'You know how he will scream if things are not to his liking'  'Who is taking fresh fruit?' the same nun asks. 'And is the meat roasted and the pastries warming.' and and and. she asks repeated questions of the nuns who nod or raise their hands in turn or reply 'Yes Sister.'  It appears everything is ready.

After finishing her hasty meal, Sister Mary passes back to the Abbot's Lodge, where she sees his carriage has pulled up outside. His two black horses still sweating in their traces. There are four mounted men at arms, they have swords at their sides, helmets and hardened leather breastplates over knee length smocks, trousers and brown leather boots. They have bows slung across their backs.  They dismount and lead their horses towards the stables.  One of the Abbots enforcers, not what anyone calls them, but what Mary considers them to be, acting as footman.  The man places a step below the carriage door and the Abbot forces his enormous bulk through the narrow carriage doorway.  The tiny step is dwarfed by his bulk, but does its job and the Abbot enters his quarters.  Mary hurries in through a side door and busies herself, ensuring the fires are all fully primed with new logs.

  'What time did you light these fires Sister Mary?' asks the Abbot as he sees her working.  'Hours ago your Holiness,' she replies.  'I feel a chill in the air,' he states 'make sure it is done earlier next time, or I will have you cleaning the latrines.' he pronounces in his nasal tone.  He shrugs his fur trimmed robes round his shoulders and turns to sample the tray of meats on the table.  Either they are adequate, or there is no one in view to criticise.  'You may leave,' he waves dismissively to the de-facto footman.  'Inform Brother Geofrey that I will be at the Chapter house within the hour to enlighten him on the new business I have been able to negotiate.' To Mary he says. 'Sister, bring warm water and a cloth, I wish to freshen up.' Mary already has water warming above a fire and a bowl and cloth ready. As she moves to take this through into the Abbots bedchamber he lets out a howl 'Waaaaaarght. Where. Mary,' he screams. She hurries in. 'Yes, your holiness, how may I serve?' she humbly asks. 'Get the Brothers,' he screams, 'All those who serve in my inner circle.' Mary hurries out. The Abbot begins searching his quarters, throwing furniture aside, pulling tapestries and curtains to the floor, throwing bedding and tipping the heavy bed upside down. Tom is surprised at the strength of the obese Abbot.

A group of six monks quickly enter. They are astonished at the sight of the red faced sweating Abbot. 'It's gone he screams. Everything we have worked for these last three years, hundreds of pounds of gold. It's all gone. Who was on gate security these last two days. We must search the entire Abbey organise teams, but ensure someone we trust is in charge of each group. I want to know of everyone who has been in my quarters these last two days. I want to know who has been working where, while I have been gone.' He holds up the earring that Sister Mary had planted. 'I found this in my chamber. Find who owns it's partner and I think we may have our thief.'

The monks file out, except for one who moves to speak with the Abbot discretely. 'Your Holiness,' he whispers. Tom and Chris drift closer. 'You asked me to watch that trouble maker Brother Peter. I suspect he may be involved in the disappearance of your chest. I saw him enter your Lodge at dusk yesterday. He was there for only a short time before returning to his quarters, but he may know something.' 'You have provided a great service my brother.' replies the Abbot 'Sadly, it would appear Brother Peter has suffered a fall from grace. Have him taken to the prison cell and ask Brother Maynard to extract his confession by whatever means necessary.'
The spy turns and scurries out of the room.

The Abbot takes a seat and begins eating.  It is not long before a nervous looking nun arrives.  'Your holiness,' she begins, wringing her hands nervously.  'I am responsible for housekeeping and if any task no matter how small has not been completed to your satisfaction, then I will ensure that......'  'I need to know who has been working in my Lodge,' interrupts the Abbot.  'I am especially interested to know who was working here at dusk yesterday.'  'That would be Sister Mary your holiness,' a relieved look on her face as she bobs a curtsey.  'Will that be all, your holiness.'  'Have sister Mary sent to me,' he demands.  'At once.'  'Yes, your holiness.'  The nun curtseys once again and hurries out of the lodge.

Sister Mary is the next person to arrive.  She looks flustered, as if she has run all the way.  'Your holiness, how may I be of service?'  'Oh, that's very simple Mary, you can tell me who came into my lodge at dusk yesterday and removed a chest from my quarters.' he replies in a charming voice.  'I'm sorry, your holiness, but I don't understand, I was working alone yesterday.  There was not much work to do, what with your important visit.' replies Mary anxiously.

 'You know Sister Mary, I have always liked you, since the day you arrived. I had hoped we could have become friends.' God he is smarmy thinks Tom. 'Which is why it saddens me all the more to think that you might lie to me. You know that Satan is the father of all lies and that your soul is at risk of eternal damnation.' intones the Abbot. 'I know full well what I do father and I have faith that the lord will receive me.' Mary clutches her hands together, drops to her knees and looks up to the heavens. 'But Mary,' says the Abbot. 'The ninth commandment is thou shalt not lie. God will not have you if you break his commandments, they are his first and most important guidance to us.' 'Father, I know my bible as I know my heart and you shall not deceive me. What has happened is a punishment upon you for your most sinful ways. The ninth commandment is, Thou shalt not bear false witness upon thy neighbour, and should I reveal the identity of my visitor, I would surely have done that.'

'You condemn yourself out of your own mouth,' replies the Abbot. 'I know you were visited by Brother Peter, as we are speaking, Peter will be telling Brother Maynard everything he knows.  Brother Maynard can be very persuasive.'  Mary hangs her head in defeat and is silent.  'So you might as well tell me where he put my chest.' continues the Abbot.  'Things will go much easier on you if you co-operate with me.  I might even be able to forget about this sorry little incident and send you back to your convent with a glowing report.'  'I would be a poor servant of god if I bowed to evil when first it rears its ugly head.' states Sister Mary, looking the Abbot square in the eye.

'So, you think me evil,' screams the Abbot.  'I will show you just what I am capable of.'  He steps towards Mary, slaps her to the floor with his puffy bejewelled hand and then grabs a handful of her robe, which judging by the noise Sister Mary makes, must include a large chunk of her hair.  He strides across the room dragging Mary behind him and proceeds up the stairs.  Mary struggles to get her feet under her, using her hands as much as her feet as she is forcibly dragged behind. Tom and Chris are compelled to follow, drifting up the stairs behind. The Abbot pulls a door open and throws Mary inside.

Tom recognises the room beyond, he saw it from a different perspective, but he has seen it before. It is a simple guest room with basic wooden furniture, a bed, a desk, a wardrobe and a soot blackened fireplace.

'You need time to contemplate Sister Mary. The church needs its chest of gold back. How will I present alms to the poor on Sunday. You are denying the needy their respite. I will be back within the hour, I hope you will be more co-operative upon my return.' He exits the room and selecting a large key from a cord around his waist, he locks the door. Tom and Chris float through the door. They have no need to follow the Abbot, Tom at least knows exactly where he is going. Mary is not curled up on the floor sobbing as they had expected, but has composed herself and is knelt in prayer. Tom turns to his brother. Chris has a mournful expression on his face and tears are flowing from his fiery eyes. 'We have to help her,' urges Tom. 'We have to get her out of here.' 'We are too late,' replies Chris in a mournful tone. 'She died over seven hundred years ago.' 'But there must be something we can do,' argues Tom. 'You brought us here, why did you do that. You have powers, break the door down so she can escape. You know the Abbot is going to wall her up if you don't.' 'Do you want to help her Thomas,' asks the ghost 'with all your heart.' 'Yes, yes,' screams Tom, 'anything.'

Over an hour passes before the Abbot returns. All this time Sister Mary continues praying. By the time he arrives Tom and Chris are gone.

## Chapter 9

It's cold. The wind is blowing and Tom and
Chris are still wearing only their boxers. They
are stood on a muddy trail through the
woods. Chris's eyes no longer have a fiery
glow and they are most definitely not as
insubstantial as ghosts. Chris looks around in
confusion 'Where are we, how did I get
here,' he stammers. 'I was in bed, I went to
bed, how did I get here, where are we.' 'The
ghost brought us here,' says Tom 'but I don't
know where here is. I said I wanted to help
Sister Mary and all of a sudden we appeared
here.' 'It's cold,' says Chris 'we need to find
some clothes. We only have two choices, left
or right.' They chose right and hobble up the
trail, doing their best to avoid stones.

They had been moving for only a few
minutes, when a girl, about their own age,
appears from around a bend in front of them.
She is carrying a wicker basket on her back,
has a white woollen shawl across her
shoulders and a blue dress that drops to her
knees. She is dirty, but still pretty, with long
brown hair framing her face. She is barefoot

like them. They try to duck into the woods to hide from her, but it is too late, they have been spotted.  She giggles, covers her mouth and briefly looks away, but then looks back and can't seem to take her eyes off them as she approaches.

 'Oh my,  It is Puck and one of his elves, play no tricks on this poor peasant girl oh fairies of the wood.'  says the girl in a plaintive tone. 'I'm no fairy' says Tom 'we're lost.  Do you know where we are.'  The girl dissolves into gales of laughter.  'Oh you are, you are and most beautiful ones too,  have you come to tempt me with your wanton pagan ways.' She steps in close towards Tom, places a hand on his shoulder and runs it seductively down across his chest and stomach. As her hand reaches the top of his boxers Tom takes a step back, catches his heel on a root and sits with a splat in a muddy puddle.  This causes the girl to giggle again.  'Oh, a shy little elf, I'm sorry.'  She reaches out a hand and pulls him too his feet.  She is surprisingly strong and she pulls Tom into a clinch.  'I'm sorry, I was only having some fun with you and look I have got you all muddy, let me clean you off.'  She hugs him tight to her and with her spare hand reaches round and begins to rub Tom's buttocks in a most ineffectual way.  Tom catches hold of both the girls arms and firmly but gently pushes her out to arms length.  She pouts and folds her arms.  'I'm only being friendly,' she says 'all the boys round here are so ugly and I'm sure that I'll be made to marry some fat old farmer before winter, you can't blame a girl for wanting a bit of fun.'  'Married,' says Chris 'You can't be more than fourteen.  You can't get married when your fourteen.'  'Shows what you know,' she replies  'my sister was married at twelve and had a baby of her own by my age.'

 'Can you help us,' interrupts Tom  'we're lost and need some clothes.'   'Well, as far as being lost goes, you are on the road from Netley village to the Abbey.  I don't have any spare clothes, but there is a woodsman's hut not far from here, you can shelter there.  Where are you from and what manner of loin cloth are you wearing.  I have never seen so brightly coloured and outlandish underwear, are you jesters and this part of your motley?'

'We are from a long way away' says Tom 'A brightly coloured land called PRIMARK, everyone who goes to PRIMARK will return dressed this way.'  'You must have travelled for many days,' she says  'I have never heard of PRIMARK.  How did you come to lose your clothes?'   'We were set upon in the night by ghosts,' replies Tom  'We went to sleep fully clothed on the high road between PRIMARK and er TESCO and woke to find ourselves lost in these woods.'  'It would appear,' giggles the girl  'that rather than being fairies, you would be the victims of such mischievous sprites.  Follow me.'

She leads them off through the woods after first collecting her basket of kindling from the forest floor. They arrive shortly at a ramshackle wattle and daub hut, with a thatched roof.  The entrance way is so low they have to stoop to enter and is covered with a muddy and ragged fur.  There are no windows and inside it is dark.  There is a small hearth and a pallet in the corner covered with a straw mattress.  There is a heap of dirty blankets piled on the mattress and there is a pile of logs beside the hearth.

There is a single pot hanging over the fire. 'Told you there was blankets,' she states proudly. 'I'll get a fire going.' She quickly stacks some of her kindling into a small wigwam shape and then pulls a quaint wooden box from below her dress. She removes punk, tinder and a flint and steel from the box and within five minutes has a cheery blaze burning, which quickly warms the small hut. Tom and Chris sit on the straw mattress with their knees pulled up to their chins and a blanket wrapped round their shoulders. The blankets are filthy and itchy, but warm and the boys are glad to have them.

I'm Tom by the way and this is my brother Chris. What's your name?' The girl introduces herself as Alice. 'I need to get back home she says, I am expected before dark.' The boys glance towards the doorway, it is already turning dusky outside. 'We need to get to the Abbey,' says Tom 'Before the Abbot returns.' 'I didn't think you were from around here,' questions Alice 'How do you know the Abbot is away.' 'Oh, the Abbot is well known,' replies Tom 'Even the Bishop of Winchester speaks highly of him.  PRIMARK is the other side of Winchester.' 'So, you're friends of the Abbot are you,' says Alice, her friendly tone suddenly turned frosty.  'No, no,' replies Tom, 'we don't know him at all, but a friend of ours may be in trouble at the Abbey, so we were travelling there to help her.' 'So, who is your friend at the Abbey?' she asks, still none too kindly.  'It's Sister Mary,'  says Tom. 'Ah, she is a good soul and worthy of your help.  The Abbot will not be back till after midday tomorrow, but it will be dark within the hour. I will take you there at first light, but now I have to go.  I will try to return later with some food.

  'Why do we have to get to the Abbey,' asks Chris  'Surely we want to stay away from there, according to Brother Peter's diary, it is a den of thieves.'  'We're here to help Sister Mary.' replies Tom   'Brother Peter wants us to rescue her before the Abbot can wall her up.'   Tom continues to explain what has happened, while Chris was possessed by the ghost and exactly why they have to get to Mary and warn her before the Abbot returns.

'Can't we warn Brother Peter as well,' asks Chris. 'Don't see why not,' replies Tom, 'Maybe he'll tell us where he buried the treasure.' The boys stoke the fire with a hefty log which they hope will last the night and curl up to sleep.

Tom is woken yet again. Fortunately, it is not a ghost this time. 'Hello Tom, I'm back.' It's Alice, she has joined them in the bed, she is laid behind him, her body pressed firmly up against his back. Her arm is wrapped around him and she is once again stroking his chest. Tom decides to leave her to it and quickly drops off to sleep again.

In the morning, they find Alice has provided breakfast, in the form of bread and cheese and apples, which they all hungrily scoff. 'Thanks Alice, that was great.' says Tom appreciatively. 'I suppose you didn't manage to get us any clothes.' 'Sorry,' replies Alice 'I told you we don't have much to spare, but if you are going to the Abbey, you could plead at the Almshouse they often give out clothing as well as food. It depends who is on duty. Sister Mary often used to work there, but not so much recently.' 'Can you lead us back to the path and point us in the right direction,' asks Chris. 'Oh and can we keep the blankets too.' 'I can do better than that,' says Alice 'I will come with you to the Almshouse and introduce you, then I can have my blankets back. They don't grow on trees you know.' Tom smiles 'Pleased to have you along Alice,' and gives her an exuberant hug.

They trudge barefoot, shrouded in blankets through the early morning mist. 'So, where do you live Alice,' asks Tom. 'Oh, down by the water. My father has a small fishing boat. We mostly live off Bass, Flounders and Eel, though we do manage to trade for eggs and bread. I also manage to collect fruit and mushrooms whilst out collecting wood.' 'Is that your job then, collecting wood,' says Tom. 'My job is helping my mother around the house, until the day I get married and then I have to do the same for my husband. What do you do.' 'Were still at school,' says Chris. 'Really, both of you, wow, you must be rich. What are you studying. Are you going to be monks, they have to read and write in Latin and English.' gushed Alice

excitedly.' 'I was thinking of being a boat builder,' says Tom 'I like boats.' 'Really, but you can read and write, you could do anything.  My dad knows a bit of boat building and he can't read a word.  Why would you want to be a boat builder, when you can read.  You could be a scribe or a clerk, or if you were really good a bailiff or chamberlain, have you no ambition.'  'Says the girl who wants to be a house wife.' chides Chris.  'I would love to be a midwife and help to deliver babies, but the local midwife has a girl who helps her and won't take another, besides, mum needs me.'  The boys didn't feel they could explain their choices, without talking about time travel and ghostly magic. They didn't want her thinking they were witches or warlocks, so they kept quiet.
 Chapter 10

 Soon, the Abbey hove into view.  The boys recognised some parts of the building, from their familiarity with the ruin, but there were many other parts, that they realized were completely absent in the future.  For starters, the first thing they were greeted with was a large gatehouse entranceway.  There is a narrow roadway leading under an arch and supporting towers either side. A wooden gate stands open under the arch. Alice marches up to a small doorway, set into the tower wall under the arch and knockes politely. A small man in a smock, with long greasy hair opens the door, he doesn't look at all like a monk. 'Hello Alice. What brings you here, more apples to sell.' he greets them. 'Not likely,' says Alice 'The Abbot pays the worst prices. He expects me to donate my goods for the glory of god, which I wouldn't mind, except it seems to me that it goes to the glory of his belly.' The doorman laughs. 'You need to be careful Alice. The wrong person hears you speaking like that and you'll get a knock on the door in the middle of the night that you won't enjoy. Anyway, who do you have here, wrapped up like a pair of lepers.' 'Travellers,' replies Alice brightly and then, as if letting him in on a big secret, she sidles closer. 'They was attacked by bandits,' she states 'striped they were and left for dead in nothing but their breeches.' 'That must have been a shocking sight for someone of your tender years,' laughs the doorman. 'You don't know the half of it,' laughs Tom. 'So what brings you here?' asks the gatekeeper. 'Alms,' says Alice. ' They need clothing and food, to continue their journey.' 'I suspect we can help with that, but you may have to help with the elderly first, the sisters at the Almshouse will be feeding the frail ones right now.'

  The boys follow Alice through the gate. They recognise the Chapel  at the back of the complex and the Abbot's Lodge off to their right in the distance, but there is also a whole mess of wooden houses, huts and gardens in front of the stone built chapel buildings.  He recognises the kitchens from the smells emanating from within, which make his stomach rumble.  Alice leads them to the Almshouse.  It is a large stone built complex, which upon entry, reminds the boys of a coffee morning at the local community centre,  except there are a lot more nuns, the old people look considerably more frail and of course, there is no coffee.  The nuns are feeding the most frail, others are able to feed themselves and some of the elderly are helping out, doing what work they are still capable of.  One of the nuns notices their entrance and waves them over.  Alice once again explains their story and the nun points them towards a pile of what looks like brown coloured rags sitting on a table in the corner.

 'Oh my god,' whispers Chris  'These are gross and they stink.'  'Beggars can't be choosers,' replies Tom as he starts to rummage through the tattered pile of clothing.  Eventually, they find a pair of smocks, which only have a few holes.  They tie these in at the waist with some off-cuts torn from another unrecognisable rag.  They are then provided with some of the gruel, which is being spoon fed to the invalids.  Alice seems quite happy with her extra helping of breakfast.  Tom and Chris less so, but they still finish their meagre helping, not knowing where their next meal might come from or how they are going to get back to their own world.  'We need to find Sister Mary,' whispers Tom after they have finished their breakfast.  'We also have to work,' states Alice, 'to repay their kindness.'

  The children are given the job of clearing and scrubbing the tables and washing the dishes.  They are finished within an hour and Alice bids them fair well, explaining that she was expected back with her load of wood ages ago.  'Hope you don't get in too much trouble on our account, just tell your parents how grateful we were for your assistance.' Tom gives her a kiss before she leaves.  The chapel bell informs them that it is 9 am.  They had been working under the supervision of one of the younger nuns, who seems quite friendly, so Tom says 'Excuse me for asking, but we need to speak to a nun called Sister Mary, is she here.'  'She is not on duty in the Almshouse' answers the nun, but I could probably find her for you.  What do you need to see her for.'  Tom hesitates, so Chris interrupts 'We have an important message for her from her family.' states Chris.  'Then I shall be happy to pass it on.' says the nun. 'Oh but it is grave news,' replies Chris in his most sombre voice.  'We really need to speak to her personally.'  'That is sad.  I will find her for you.' says the nun and hurries off.

  The nun returns within ten minutes.  'Sister Mary will be here within the hour,' states the nun.  'She has duties she must complete

first.'  'We can't afford to wait too long,'
whispers Chris, 'if the Abbot gets back before
we are well away...'  He doesn't need to finish
his sentence, Tom knows exactly what will
happen.  'Let's sneak out and find her,' says
Tom.  'If my vision is correct, she should be
cleaning and laying fires in the Abbot's Lodge
by now.'  'If anyone asks, we can tell them
we are looking for the toilets,' says Tom.

  The boys leave the Almshouse and hurry
towards the main chapel complex.  They skirt
round the outside of portions of the Abbey
that don't exist in their time and past the
kitchens, refectory and warming room.  They
can now see the Abbot's Lodge, the other
side of the gardens.  They cross a vegetable
patch, with what they believe to be the
toilets and infirmary to their left.  'That's
where the tunnel runs through,' comments
Tom as they hurry past.  They reach the
Abbot's Lodge unchallenged and knock on
the door.

  The door is answered by a nun, that Tom
instantly recognises as Sister Mary.  'Sister
Mary,' he says, 'you don't know me, but my

name is Tom.  My brother and I are here to help you.' 'That's very kind of you,' replies Mary, confused 'but it really is unnecessary, there is very little to do here, what with the Abbot being away.' 'We're not here to help with the housework,' states Tom, 'Your life is in danger.  We are here to help you and Brother Peter get away from this place.' Sister Mary looks nervously over their heads and to either side. 'You had better come in,' she says.  She ushers them inside, shuts the door firmly and turns sharply to the boys. 'You had better tell me what you think you know and quickly, I have no time for little boys playing practical jokes.'  Tom looks her straight in the eye and simply states.  'You and Brother Peter stole the Abbots gold last night.  Before the day is out he will be torturing Brother Peter and you will be locked up in the guest room upstairs.' 'Where did you get this ridiculous story,' replies Mary, 'I don't know where you boys get your ideas for your silly games,' but she is looking nervous wringing the cloth in her hands. 'Mary, we are here to help you.  The earring you leave on the floor does not fool anyone.  We know everything and if you don't leave with us now, you will get walled up in the hearth of the guest room upstairs and left there to die.'

'I believe you,' says Mary. 'I fear that you may have used witchcraft to know the future and the past so accurately, but you don't look like witches or warlocks. I think I must trust you, but what can I do. I have nowhere to go, this is my home.' 'First we have to find Brother Peter and get away from here. We know a hut in the woods where we can hide. We can make further plans once we are there.' 'I don't know where Brother Peter will be right now, it will take me time to find him. You should wait here, out of sight while I look for him.' 'It's best if we don't stay here,' says Tom, 'I think the Abbot has someone watching the lodge, that's how he knows Brother Peter was here last night. Is there somewhere else we can hide.' 'I will take you across to the monks reredorter. It's above the infirmary, alongside the monks dorter. You can hide in Brother Peters cubicle. Each monk has their own and they are separated by screens. So long as you stay quiet in there, no one will find you.' 'What's a reredorter,' asks Chris. 'It's where the monks do their private business,' replies Mary, with a slight blush. 'Oh, right,' mumbles Chris, 'A bit like an office then?' The boys follow Mary out the back door of the Abbot's Lodge. They swing round the side, from where they can see the infirmary door.

'See the door there,' says Mary. 'Go through it, turn right and go up the first stairs you come to, turn left at the top and the reredorter will be in front of you. Peters cubicle is the one at the very end on the left.' The boys jog across to the infirmary door, trying to look like messengers, who know where they are going. The infirmary only has two patients and they hurry past, the Sisters working there are either too busy to notice, or too busy to care, what the two boys are up to and they pass unchallenged. The staircase is a narrow stone spiral, wide enough for one person only. At the top they turn left and enter the reredorter. They head towards the end cubicle, which, like all the others, has a tattered curtain hanging across the entrance. 'This doesn't look like an office,' queries

Chris. 'It's the bogs isn't it.' 'Yes, now keep quiet. I don't want to be caught hiding in here with you.' whispers Tom. Just as he finishes speaking, they hear hurried footsteps and a voice saying 'Oh god, Oh god, Oh god please.' 'I don't think he's praying,' whispers Tom as an explosive fart and a splattering noise fills the room. 'Do you think he made it.' smirks Tom. 'I hope so,' replies Chris, 'We may have to be here for some time.' They hear many grunts and groans and curses, before the monk eventually staggers back towards the dorter.

  They sit hunched up on the wooden cover, either side of the long drop to the drainage channel, which they guess must be at least thirty feet below. There is a board covering the hole and fortunately, Brother Peter kept his cubicle very clean, so the wait was not too unpleasant. After his initial visit, the farty monk returns only once more and no other monks visit the reredorter before Brother Peter draws back the curtain. He does not look happy. 'You have told Sister Mary an incredible story and have got her very worried.' he says, not giving anything away.

'I have given her a factual account of exactly what you and her did last night,' replies Tom. 'I could repeat the story, including how you bought a sailors earring in Woolston, to try and divert attention away from yourselves, but I really don't think we have time.  The Abbot will be back by noon and the pair of you will be in a cell shortly after.  We need to leave now.  We also can't talk much longer, a fellow monk of yours is visiting regularly with a stomach problem.'

  Brother Peter pauses, takes a breath, as if to argue and then appears to make a decision. 'Wait here,' he says, 'while I collect a few things.'  'Be discrete,' says Tom.  'You don't want anyone knowing that you're leaving.'

## Chapter 11

Brother Peter disappears quietly into the dorter and returns within a few minutes. They follow him down the stairs and out the infirmary door. 'Sister Mary is going to meet us in one of the gardens. Most of the Brothers will be in the Cloister or Chapter House at this time, so all we will come across are lay brothers or villagers who work here, neither of which will challenge us.' They skirt round the edge of the Abbey, discretely avoiding any groups of workers and staying well away from the Cloister and Chapter house. They quickly make it to the gardens, but Mary is nowhere to be seen. There is only one nun in sight and she is busy digging vegetables and dropping them into a basket. They make their way in her direction, but are unsure whether to ask about Sister Mary. The more people who see them depart, the more people who can provide information later. Fortunately, as they get closer, the busy worker raises her head and they see that it is Sister Mary. The clever woman was hiding in plain sight and had also gathered some food for their journey.  If you enjoy carrots and cabbage, that is.

  'Follow me,' says Sister Mary.  She lifts the basket, places her arms through straps and settles it on her back.  She leads them along a narrow pathway and through a gate in a wattle fence into an apple orchard.  They continue through the orchard in silence until they reach a track through the forest on the far side.  'We should be safe here for a while,' says Mary,  'but where to now?'  Brother Peter turns towards the twins and asks, 'Do you know why we took the gold?'   'Because,' says Chris, 'The Abbot is evil and he has been over taxing the local people for years, which has made them very poor.  You want to give the gold to the people who need it most.' 'You are  correct,' says Brother Peter, which means we need to hide out close by.  I can then distribute at least a portion of the gold, before we depart.'   'We could take the rest with us,' says Sister Mary, 'and set up an Almshouse when we are far from here.'  'We met a fisherman's daughter, who may be able to take us across the water,' says Tom.  'That will make it harder for anyone to follow.  You could then get some ponies on the other side.'  They decide to make their way back to the hut in the woods and hide there, after which, Tom can make his way down to the shoreline to find Alice and her father's boat. Tom describes the track they travelled to reach the Abbey.  'What if the Abbot comes down that trail,' says Chris, 'We could walk straight into him.'  Neither Brother Peter, nor Sister Mary have any idea where the Abbots business trip had taken him or which route he might be taking to return to the Abbey. Then Tom has an idea.  'I suggest we follow the track but don't actually walk on it.  If we stay a few hundred yards back in the woods, we can parallel it and have plenty of time to duck down and hide if the Abbot should come along.  It will make for a slow journey, but will be safer, until we are far away from here.'

  They all agreed to the plan.  Progress is slow, diverting around brambles, pushing through ferns that are waist high and climbing around and through fallen trees. Despite the noise of their progress, they easily spot first a lone horseman passing along the track and later a wagon heading towards the Abbey.  Each time, they quickly duck down behind bushes and remain still and silent until the traveller has long passed before once more emerging.  They continue steadily in this way until they hear a group of horsemen and a carriage approaching.  It is the Abbot.  With hammering hearts they hit the floor like sacks of grain dropped from a hayloft.  They lie still as statues, afraid to breath.  They keep their faces flat to the floor and listen to the horses hooves and the jingle of the carriage as it moves closer and closer.

  Eventually, the carriage draws level and begins to disappear towards the Abbey. Their heart rate begins to drop and finally they manage to draw a full breath.  The Abbot has passed and they are safe.  'Don't move until we can't hear them anymore,' whispers Brother Peter.  They lie still, listening carefully as the sounds start to fade. They think they are safe, when they hear a voice call out.

  'Your Holiness, stop, I must speak with you. It is I, Brother Maynard.'  The coach quickly comes to a halt and the Abbot's head appears out the window. 'You ordered me to watch Brother Peter. He is here. He is running away from the Abbey with a nun and two boys helping him. He was in your Lodge last night.' 'Get after him, stop him,' shouts the Abbot,' 'show my men where.' 'Follow me,' shouts Brother Maynard. He gathers his robes up to his waist and runs down the track, his white legs flashing above his sandaled feet. The four mounted men at arms turn their horses and gallop back down the trail after him. 'Over there,' shouts Brother Maynard, as the horsemen catch up to him, pointing out into the woodland.

Brother Peter and his entourage are already up and running. The horsemen plunge down game trails, their helmets and shoulders crashing through branches as they hunch low over their mounts. The runners only have a short head start, the dense undergrowth is to their advantage, but the horsemen are still closing fast. Tom and Chris break out into a clearing, with horsemen closing in on a wide front, they have no choice but to dash across it and hope they can reach cover in the woods the far side, before the horsemen close in.  Sister Mary is caught first.  She has already dropped her basket, to aid her running, but it is not enough.  As she breaks through into the clearing, she is struggling to keep up with the others.  A horseman comes alongside her and grabs her habit as he rides past.  This is enough to drag Sister Mary off her feet and she hits the ground hard.

'Stop or I shoot,' shouts the lead horseman. Chris has almost reached the other side of the clearing when he hears the call.  It reminds him of every lousy American cop show he has ever watched.  No one ever stops in these shows and no one is ever hit, despite bullets being sprayed everywhere. He keeps going until he hears a scream from behind.  Tom hears the shout too.  He is a big fan of all the old A Team shows and knows from watching them, that if someone runs in a zigzag, it is almost impossible to hit them. He swaps the angle of his run and after six paces changes direction again.  He hears a bow twang and expects to see the arrow come whizzing over his head.

He is most surprised, therefore, when a punch hits him in the middle of the back. It reminds him of when Casey had fouled him at football and he had been smashed flat on his back, all the wind knocked out of him. He had lain on the grass gasping for breath for at least five minutes, cursing his erstwhile friend, when he had finally been able to. This blow knocked him forward and it took some fancy footwork just to stay on his feet, this he managed for about two more steps, before looking down and seeing the arrow protruding from his chest. He tries to draw a breath, but it is agony. He knows he is going to fall. He twists sideways as he goes down, trying not to land on the protruding arrow. As he hits the floor, everything goes black. The last thing he hears is his brother screaming his name in a long drawn out panic stricken screech.'

Chris reaches the shelter of the woodland on the far side of the clearing. He stops, gasping for breath, leaning briefly against a tree trunk before looking back towards the others. Sister Mary is caught, a horseman dismounted alongside her. One horseman is stopped on the edge of the meadow, his bow drawn fully back.  There is only one other rider visible and he has his sword drawn.  He has caught Brother Peter halfway across the field and before Chris has a chance to shout a warning the sword flashes down and strikes Brother Peter across the back of the head.  The swordsman has used the side of the blade, so it is not a killing blow.  He still hears the clang of steel on bone and sees an explosion of blood as Brother Peters scalp is split and he collapses to the floor unmoving.  Almost simultaneously he hears the bow string release and looks to see the arrow streaking unerringly towards his brother.

'Tom,' he screams as he runs back towards him.  Chris throws himself on his knees beside his brother.  'Tom, Tom, come on get up, you're all right, we have to keep running.  You can't be dead, I love you.'  Tears are flooding down Chris's cheeks, he knows that his brother is dead.  He falls back sits on his heels and looks up at the sky.  A scream of abject misery rents the air.  'Nooooo.  Toooom.'  The scream is cut short, as a second arrow explodes through his throat.  It hits with such force, that it passes right through and hits the ground well beyond the falling body.  Chris is dead before his body hits the floor.

## Chapter 12

'Tooooom.' The scream is long and drawn out. It is a scream of misery. A scream of fear. A scream of pain. Tom jerks awake in a panic to find Chris sitting bolt upright on the side of his bed. His head thrown back looking up at the ceiling, screaming his name at the top of his lungs. Then, his whole body jerks as if hit by an electric shock and Chris slumps to the floor. Tom scrambles out of bed and drops to the floor beside his stricken brother. He rolls him over. Chris's eyes are wide open, unblinking, staring straight up at him. They are no longer the possessed fiery eyes of Blind Peter, but they are lifeless and dull.

Tom grabs his twin by the shoulders, afraid, that when he touches his brother, his body will be as cold as dead meat. He shakes him and calls his name.

Chris blinks and life floods back into his eyes. He looks at Tom. 'You were dead.' he says. 'An arrow stuck straight through your chest.'

Before Tom can reply, there is a crash as the bedroom door is thrown open. 'Christ on a bike,' shrieks their dad. 'I thought someone was being murdered. What the hell are you shouting about?' 'I had a nightmare,' quavers Chris 'I thought Tom was dead.' 'What are you doing on the floor,' asks their dad. 'I don't know,' replies Chris. 'I just woke up here.' tears of confusion and shock burst from his eyes and Chris begins to shudder and sob. Dad scoops him up from the floor and sits on Toms bed hugging Chris to him. 'Hey, it's okay, it's only a nightmare, it's not real. It can't hurt you.' Dad rubs his back and strokes the hair back from his face. Tom quietly joins in the hug. If nightmares can't hurt you, he thinks, then why can he still feel the place where the arrow burst out of his chest. He shudders at the thought, as if someone has walked over his grave. Tom thinks back to the last time his dad had hugged him. It was bed time and Casey had been sleeping over. His dad had given him a hug and a bedtime kiss, one of the over exaggerated, farty, slobbery kisses he does for comic effect, when he is afraid of showing affection. Tom had told him off for embarrassing him and insisted he was too old for hugs and kisses. That had been over a

year ago.  His dad had taken him at his word.
Tom looked at his dad.  'You know what I said
about hugging.  Well I think it's ok if you do it
sometimes, just not in front of my friends.'
His dad smiled and hugged him even harder.
Then mum arrived.  'He was sleepwalking and
had a nightmare,' says dad.  Mum joins in the
group hug.  'Let's get you back to bed.' she
says.  'It's late and you have school in the
morning.'

  Tom can't believe it is still Sunday night.  It
feels like two whole days have passed.  Dad
carries Chris out of the room, he has one arm
under his legs and the other round his back.
Chris's head is resting on his shoulders.  His
eyes closed.  Tom slumps back onto his bed.
They were supposed to rescue Sister Mary
and they had failed.  This was not over.  Blind
Peter, he was sure, would not be happy at
their failure.  Brother Peter had seemed like a
nice, caring, friendly person, but Tom knew,
at least part of, what he had been through.
He wondered how long Peter had lived after
the Abbot had blinded him.  What
deprivations he had experienced.  He
doubted that anyone could live as a blind

servant to a devilish master and be unaffected by the experience. Tom was afraid. He had experienced torture, death and being walled up. He wondered what Blind Peter had in store for him next and what he could do to avert it. Tom dropped off to sleep, with these thoughts buzzing around his brain.

Thankfully, the remainder of his night passes uneventfully. He goes through his morning routine cautiously, watching Chris for any sign of continued ghostly possession. School passes in a blur, unable to focus on anything other than the nights events. He gets a detention for his lack of homework. The lecture about the importance of homework drifts over his head like so many cumulous clouds and the detention letter disappears into his back pocket without a glance.

By the time they get home, Tom has come up with a plan. 'We have to go back.' he insists. They are upstairs. Tom has wandered through into Chris's bedroom. Mum had received a phone call about the lack of homework and had, upon their arrival at home, immediately sent them to their rooms to get it finished. Tom had sat for a few minutes, staring at his homework before deciding to share his plan with his brother. He figures, that if Chris was still possessed, then the ghost would be pleased with the plan and might leave him alone until he was able to implement it. Even if he wasn't possessed Tom figured that there was no way he was going to put his plan into action without some back up.

'Back in time?' asks Chris. 'To try and rescue Sister Mary again? I know what we did wrong. We should have left Brother Peter. We should have remembered he was being watched. We need to be more careful, more sneaky.' 'No,' says Tom, 'I don't know how that happened, or if we could go back again, if it was real, or if it was a nightmare. But we did learn something important.' Tom pauses for dramatic effect. 'What?' prompts Chris. 'We know where Sister Mary was walled up. The guest room in the Abbot's Lodge. We can still rescue her, just seven hundred years too late. I think it would still make Blind Peter happy, if we can lay her bones to rest.'

Chris smiles.  'Yes, your right, but I still don't want to go back to the Abbey.  The last time I was there I got possessed by the ghost of Blind Peter, in case you've forgotten.'  'No.  I haven't forgotten.  That's the other reason we have to go back.  I think you're still possessed.  Your eyes were glowing again last night, before we went back in time, you took me to the Abbey, you showed me a vision of Peter and Mary stealing the chest.'  'I don't remember any of that,' says Chris.  'Did you see where it was hidden.'  'No, but it was definitely put in the tunnels.  Shame we didn't ask Brother Peter, when we had the opportunity,' says Tom.  'We only just met him Tom.  Would you tell someone where you had hidden a million quid, within an hour of meeting them, no matter how much you trusted them.  If we had started asking questions like that, he would have assumed we were spies and ditched us.  It's a good plan anyway.  If we can find Sister Mary's bones, maybe he will leave us alone.  When do you want to go, not night time, please.'

'We can go tomorrow, after school, but before it gets dark.' replies Tom. 'We might have to hang around until no one is about though. If we get there for seven thirty, it won't get dark until nine. It was the middle of May and although it wasn't exactly warm yet, the summer solstice was only about a month away, which meant the evenings were already stretching out. If we find anything, we clear off and then call the Police from a phone box on the way home.

'Can't we go earlier,' asks Chris nervously. 'Not unless you want to miss swimming.' replies Tom. Tuesday night was Scout swimming. Their troop were National Champions, so if they wanted to retain the trophy they were expected to attend swimming every week. The Gala consisted of a team of 12 swimming in four age groups. They were part of the U14 team each would swim an individual event, a medley relay and a squadron relay with the U12 swimmers. Chris was down to swim breast stroke, while Tom was doing front crawl. Chris was better at both, but felt his chances of a win were better at breast stroke. 'Can't do that, Skip would kill us.' They knew the Skipper of the

Scouts wouldn't have a go at them, but he would be disappointed. Neither of them were keen to disappoint him. Sea Scouts was one of the best things in their lives and had given them so many opportunities. At the age of thirteen, they could handle just about any boat on the river and were particularly keen kayakers. Their dad had told them that if they could learn to Eskimo roll he would buy them a kayak. Skip had taught them both to roll that spring. Dad had been true to his word, though it had taken him a while to find them at the right price on ebay. 'Nah, your right, we can't miss swimming.' agrees Chris, 'but we need to go straight away afterwards.'

It's seven forty five. They have hidden their bikes behind the church and hiked down the hill to the fence round the Abbey. Tom lays on his belly and pushes his backpack through the hole. He then wriggles through after it, briefly snagging the back of his jeans on the wire. The backpack has his swimming kit, but also a torch, hammer and chisel. Chris follows after, he has left his swimming kit with the bikes. Once through the fence, they skirt along it, trying to stay in the shadows of the bushes and trees around the perimeter. Once they have the Abbot's Lodge between them and the wardens house, they dart across to the back of the ruined building. There are three large holes in the back of the lodge and also a square, well like structure, where the Abbots Latrine come waste chute had been.  The square wall is uneven and broken in places.  Like the rest of the Abbey, it is made of grey unevenly cut stones mortared in place.  The boys lean against the wall and look down the hole.  There is a slightly more modern structure embedded in the walls, just below the lip of the drop.  A large iron grid has been placed there to prevent anyone accidentally falling in.  'Look at all the rubbish,' says Chris.  There are mountains of it, but also many coins can be clearly seen glittering amongst the tin cans, crisp packets and other less recognisable rubbish.  'Some idiots will use anything as a wishing well.' replies Tom.  'We could have got all of that if I hadn't been possessed by Blind Peter,' says Chris.  'Yeah, all of five pounds.  Well worth risking your life for.' agrees Tom sarcastically.   'I will just be happy if we can get rid of that ghost.  Come on, this way.'

  Tom leads his brother to a rocky climb up the edge of a broken wall.  It is a relatively simple climb and one they have both done before.  The first floor of the Abbot's Lodge consists of very little.  The outer walls are relatively intact.  The floor has no holes and has a protective coating on it, to prevent water ingress from collapsing the ceilings below.  All the interior walls are long gone, but there are the remains of two chimneys.  There is no sign of where the original staircase would have accessed the area.  Both chimneys have fire places that have been bricked up, but one seems to have been done far more recently than the other.  'This looks like the most likely place,' says Tom, pointing to the older of the two pieces of brickwork.  'This is gonna make some noise, keep a look out.'

  Chris makes his way to one of the lower parts of the wall and looks out across the Abbey ruins.  To his left, the last rays of the days sunshine are still poking their way through the branches of the tallest trees. In front of him only the single arch of the tallest point of the Abbey is still bathed in its glow. He scans the shadows carefully looking for movement. 'Looks clear,' he whispers back.

  Tom begins carefully tapping at the mortar between the stones. Although he is being slow and gentle, the sound seems to echo back off the ruined walls at an alarming volume. Chris winces at every noise, but he can see the wardens house from his lofty perch and it appears there is no one at home. At least, there are no lights on in the premises and there is no car parked on the gravel out front. The gate at the entrance way is also closed, like it usually is. This means there should be no visitors or unexpected dog walkers to interrupt their work. 'Hit it harder,' says Chris, 'There's no one around but it's going to be dark soon.' Tom ups the tempo and within a few minutes he has cleared most of the mortar around his first brick. With one hard tap, it slides back into the wall about a centimetre. After hitting it a third time, it disappears and Tom hears it fall down inside.

'I've made a hole,' says Tom. 'Can you see anything inside,' asks Chris, looking over his shoulder. Tom pulls out his torch and pokes it in the hole, but the tight angle prevents him from getting a good view to look down inside. 'I need to clear some more,' he says. 'Just smash it as hard as you can, so we can get out of here,' urges Chris as Tom again begins tapping at the mortar. 'If there is nothing in there,' states Tom, 'and we get caught smashing up a national monument, then I would like it to be possible to put the thing back together, without charging us thousands of pounds thank you.' 'Whatever,' says Chris, 'just hurry up.'

It takes Tom twenty minutes to remove another five bricks and create a hole big enough to shine a torch in and poke his head through. 'Stop working, someone's coming,' says Chris. A white transit van has pulled up at the gate. The sun has gone down and it is now fully dusk, but Chris sees one men get out and approach the gate. He has a black hoodie, jeans and trainers. He is carrying some kind of long metal bar in his hands. He steps confidently towards the gate, looks once in each direction and reaches for the chain securing the gate. Chris realises that the tool in the man's hands is a bolt cutter as he sees the chain fall loose. The man pushes the gate open so that the van can drive through, before closing the gate and hanging the chain back in place. They park the vehicle and turn the lights off. 'They cut the chain,' whispers Chris. 'They have no right to be here.' Tom looks down inside the fire place and then moves across to join his brother spying on the intruders. 'Neither do we,' he replies.

Bolt cutter man is quickly joined by the driver. It is impossible to make out any features as they are too far away and it is almost dark. The pair move to the back of the van and haul the doors open. A third person jumps out. The third member of the group is much shorter and slimmer than the first two, probably a boy. The boy is arguing with the men and then turns as if to leave. Driver grabs him by the arm, spins him around and back hands him across the face. The boy looks stunned and stands there with his head down, shoulders shaking.  He is crying.

'They are there,' says Tom 'Right where we expected them to be.'  'They shouldn't be here at all,' says Chris.  'No. The bones. Sister Mary.  She is in the fireplace, at least some bones are.  I guess the Police will be able to tell how old they are.'  Chris looks pleased, but does not take his eyes from the intruders.

## Chapter 13

The driver reaches into the back of the van. He pulls out a shovel, pick axe and crowbar. He puts a head torch on and passes another to Bolt Cutter, who also puts it in place, but neither turn the torches on.  Driver grabs the boy and frog marches him towards the front of the Abbey.  Boltcutter follows and the three of them disappear out of sight.

'We have to stop them,' says Chris 'They're after my treasure.'  His voice has taken on a cold dead tone as if his words are coming from beyond the grave.  'Are you okay Chris,' enquires his brother nervously, expecting Chris's eyes to start blazing at any moment. 'I'm still here,' answers Chris in his own voice, but I think Peter is here too.  I can feel his presence in my head.  He wants to help us. We need to follow them.'  The boys scramble back down the rocky incline at the back of the Abbot's Lodge and run towards the Chapel.  This route gives them the shortest distance to cross and the best chance of finding cover the other side, there being several rooms and walls between themselves and their intended destination.  They assume that the intruders are heading for the kitchens, beside the entrance.

  The boys enter from the rear of the chapel, where there is no wall whatsoever.  This way they have a clear field of view if the intruders are near.  They quickly cross to a point where they can look across the cloisters, without being seen.  They stay on the grass and avoid any gravelly and rocky areas, in the hope of making no noise, whilst still moving quickly.  On the far side of the cloisters, they can see light coming from the kitchen area.  The men have turned their torches on.  They can hear voices, and one of them they recognise.

  'I'm not going down there, Chris nearly died last time, that wasn't part of the deal.'  It's Casey.  He is the boy with the two men! 'Stop snivelling you wimp.  You'll do what your told and the deal is whatever I say it is.' 'Please Spider,' says Casey,  'I showed you the entrance.  We already checked the other end last time, so it's only this one tunnel.  I can stay up here and keep a lookout.  You'll need a lookout, what if someone sees the van.'

says Casey hopefully.  Clearly, Driver, otherwise known as Spider is unimpressed by Casey's appeal.  Spider is a tall gangly man, he has lank greasy unwashed dark hair and a tattoo of a spiders web, which reaches halfway across his cheek.  He is wearing skin tight jeans, baseball boots a mangy white T-shirt, covered by a sleeveless ragged Jeans jacket.  He is in his early twenties.  Bolt cutter, they recognise.  He is about eighteen and used to go to their school, a few years back.  He has a girlfriend in year eleven and is often seen hanging around outside the gates. He sells cigarettes at a pound each.  The boys suspect he also sells other things too.  His name is Bugsy, which is a classic name for a gangster, let alone a cheap hoodlum.  The boys know, however, that Bugsy is not named after Bugsy Malone.  He has a round chubby face, full of acne and has two large buck teeth.  He was nick named Bugsy at school as a shortened version of Bugs Bunny. He is a comical character, but neither of the boys would dare to laugh at him.  He is known to have a vicious streak.  The twins older sister was in the same year as Bugsy at school.  They had been warned never to buy from him, or make fun of him.  One of the other kids in her year had got in debt to him.  When Bugsy had demanded payment, an argument had started.  Bugsy had been punched and had ended up on his backside, with blood pouring from his nose, a gang of kids stood around laughing at him.  The next day, the boy who had punched him was in hospital.  The story is, that he was set upon on the way home from the skate ramps.  Two men in balaclavas and with baseball bats had broken his arm and six ribs and had given him a serious concussion.  The boy had told the Police he didn't know who had done it, but Bugsy got his money and the boy and his friends had been very polite to him ever since.

  Spider grabs Casey by the Chin, pushing his head back and digging his long fingers into his cheeks.  'You'll go down,' he snarls, 'and you'll go down first.  I'm not having you up here, where you can run off crying to mummy.'  He pushes Casey towards the wooden railing.

Casey slides over the railing quickly, eager to be away from Spider.  He disappears step by step below the level of the wall.  Bugsy goes over next, followed by spider.  As Spider passes out of sight, Chris and Tom sprint across the cloister square to the kitchen entrance.  There is still a faint glow of light splashed against the far wall above the drainage channel.

'What can we do,' asks Tom. 'We'll never stop those two, they're a right pair of nutters.'  'We have to,' says Chris, 'or they will find the treasure.  I fear they have little intention of using it for good deeds.'  Tom gives Chris a quizzical look, wondering at his odd choice of language.  'We have to get Casey away from them as well,' says Tom.
'Follow me,' says Chris. 'I have a plan.  At least, I think Peter does.'  Chris climbs into the pit and Tom reluctantly follows.  At the bottom, he gets Tom's torch out of his backpack, but does not turn it on.  Chris heads into the tunnel.  It is pitch black around them, but in the distance, there is a faint glow, from Spider and Bugsy's head torches. 'Follow me in silence,' says Chris.  'When I

start running and shouting, do the same. After I grab Casey, make sure we don't get split up.' They follow the glow of the light ahead, without turning on their torch and can soon hear voices raised in argument.

'It's dangerous though Spider. This whole tunnel is a death trap, you can see how loose some of the stones are. We could be buried alive and who knows we're here. No one, that's who.' The boys hear a loud slap. 'Calm down you div. This was your plan. If there's millions down here, then I want em.' 'Yeah, but I dint know it were gonna be like this. He just said about the chest of gold, not the water and mud and rubbish and rats and....' 'What rats,' snarls Spider 'man up, the kids got more guts than you.' Casey stands nervously to one side. 'We just have to keep checking the walls for loose rocks, It's here, I promise you. I'm not lying, we did find the old monks diary.' Casey was fervently wishing he had never mentioned the gold to Bugsy. When he couldn't afford to pay for the packet of cigarettes he had asked Bugsy to buy for him, he had carelessly boasted that he would soon have millions in gold and that then he could buy as many cigarettes as he wanted.  Not that he really wanted any at all. He was only getting them to show off in front of his older friends.  Bugsy's face had lit up with greed and his attitude had changed completely.  He had even given Casey a free cigarette, in return for telling him the whole story.  Casey had blurted the whole story.  He knew he was never going to go back to look for the treasure, but at least he could use the story to get in with Bugsy.

  Little did he suspect, that the very next day, he would be bundled into the back of a van by Spider, notorious local drug dealer and hard man.   Spider had a reputation for extreme violence and a short temper. Casey's step dad had been in the local pub one night when a fight had broken out round the pool table.  Spider had been playing pool with his missus.  A skeletally thin drug addict by the name of rose.  A group of drunkards are at a table nearby and one of them gets pushed into Spider while he is taking his shot. We'll you would have thought the world was ending.  Spider explodes in the guys face, pushes him back into his friends, snaps the pool cue over his knee and proceeds to lay into the whole group with the heavy end. He doesn't stop until all five of them are on the floor moaning, claret splashed up the walls. Spider throws the pool cue on the floor, spits on his victims, grabs his coat in one hand and Rose in the other and walks out the door. Casey's step dad claims everyone had quickly left the pub, before the Police arrived and no charges had ever been brought against Spider. Casey had asked his stepdad why he had never spoken to the Police. 'Not worth the agro. You need to pick your fights carefully,' was the only reply he had received, which Casey had interpreted as 'I was too scared. I only pick fights I know I can win.' Having met spider up close, this was an attitude that Casey could now fully understand.

 Spider had bundled him into the back of van. 'You're going to help us find your treasure.' He had snarled. 'I can't. I have to get home.' Casey had begged. A punch to the stomach had knocked all the wind out of him. 'It wasn't a question.' was all Spider had replied. Casey had lain gasping for breath on a pile of dust cloths, in amongst a load of paint cans and brushes in the back of the van. Now he was in the last place he wanted to be, back in the tunnels under the Abbey.

'Aaaaargh,' there is a blood curdling scream. 'He's right behind us. It's Blind Peter, he's gonna kill us all.' The three of them turn towards the noise to see a light bobbing and jerking towards. It's close and closing fast. 'Help! Help! It's right behind us. Please, somebody help us.' Chris and Tom burst past a startled Spider. Chris crashes into Casey, grabs hold of him and pushes him on further down the tunnel, careful not to knock him over. They continue on running. Spider has moved to block the tunnel behind them. He has the crowbar firmly clutched in both hands across his chest, ready to defend himself, he is peering into the darkness, scanning his head torch carefully back and forth. Bugsy is stood behind him clutching the shovel in an upright position above his head , blade held ready to swing down. They pause for a few seconds, which is all the boys need to disappear into the darkness. There is nothing there, there is nothing coming. 'Hey.

Where'd they go.  Come back,' shouts Spider.
'There's nothing there.'  He turns looking in
the other direction.  Trying to spot where the
boys have gone.  He sees a light in the
distance.  It is not a torch light.  It's like a
candle, no, two candles, fiery eyes coming
towards him.

  Bugsy screams ' Ruuuuun.  It's Blind Peter.'
Spider, already unnerved by the screaming
boys, makes a bolt for it.  He had heard from
Bugsy, the story of how the ghost had
possessed Chris.  He had, of course, not
believed it, but was terrified that now he
might become Blind Peters next victim.  He
remembers the old joke about two men
halfway across a bull field.  Upon seeing the
bull, one man turns to the other and says 'Do
you think you can run faster than the bull.'
No.' replies the man, 'But I don't need to.'
'How come.' asks the first man.  'Because I
can run faster than you.' he says, sprinting for
the far side of the field.  As Bugsy tries to
push past him Spider slams him into the wall
and keeps going.  For good measure, he
starts smashing his crowbar into the walls
and ceiling, trying to dislodge rocks to block

the way behind him.  He hears a scream from behind him.  'It's got me.  Aaaaargh.'  Bugsy has slumped to the floor.  He slowly climbs to his feet.  'Now I'm coming for you Spider. Your evil ways end here tonight.  Bugsy starts stumbling towards Spider, shovel raised threateningly above his head.   Spider is sure he can beat Bugsy in a fight, but is unnerved by the thought that the ghost may have lent him supernatural strength.  He backs away from Bugsy, jabbing furiously at the ceiling and walls, knocking one block after another free from the walls and ceiling.  Rocks begin falling one after another, faster and faster as he continues backing away from Bugsy. Eventually it happens, the whole ceiling slumps downward, the weight of hundreds of tons of earth has become too much for the fragile structure.  It doesn't crash down.  It is more of a cascade, which overwhelms Bugsy's possessed body.  The legs become encased up to the knee in earth and rubble. Bugsy cranes forward, scrabbling with his hands to pull himself forward as the earth continues to rain down around him.  By the time Spider turns to run, Bugsy is no longer moving.  The tunnel is completely blocked

from floor to ceiling.  The upper part of
Bugsy's torso is sticking out of a wall of earth,
which must weigh tons.  The remnants of the
collapse still trickling across his hoodie.
Bugsy is still screaming for spiders blood.  'I
will kill you all for violating my sanctuary.
This is my home.  Don't think you can escape
me.'  Spider is gone.  Sprinting down the
tunnel as fast as his legs will carry him.

  Chris sprints up the tunnel in total darkness.
He has turned the torch off, but is still
dragging Casey.  Tom is following behind,
using the noise of their passage to guide him
and running one hand along the wall to his
right to ensure he does not go off course and
run headlong into it.  After what seems like
miles, but is probably only a hundred yards,
Chris pulls them to one side and briefly flicks
the torch on.  They are in a side tunnel.
There is only a small entrance, easily missed
in the dark, but somehow he had known it
was there.  'Stop here.'  he says, 'if they are
still following us, then they will go past in the
dark and then we can run back the other
way.  He switches the torch back off, so as
not to give away their position, and they

huddle against each other listening carefully for signs of pursuit.  They don't hear anyone following, but do hear screams, which are quickly muffled and cut off, by a rumbling sound.  A puff of wind passes the tunnel and the smell of fresh earth comes with it.  They wait in silence for several minutes, straining to hear any further noises.

   'I think they're gone,' says Tom.  'Turn the torch on.'  'Spider will kill us all,' says Casey.  'Not if Blind Peter gets him first.  That was one angry ghost,' warns Chris.  'Do you think it's safe to get out of here,' asks Tom.  Chris flicks the torch on.  They all squint to get used to the light.  Tom looks down blinking and there it is, glistening on the floor, a single gold coin.  Tom drops to his knees.  'Oh my god, Oh my god we've found it. It must be here somewhere.'  He clutches the gold coin between his thumb and forefinger and thrusts it triumphantly upwards towards the light.  'Sssshh.  Spider might come back.' says Casey.  They quickly shine the light around the walls, and there at floor level is a loose stone, the glint of gold showing around its edges.  'Leave it here,' says Tom.  'If spider is still around he will steal it from us. Let's get out of here and check where he is.' He slips the coin into an inside zip pocket of his jacket, for safe keeping.

Chris leads the way cautiously back down the tunnel. He keeps the torch on, but listens carefully, ready to switch it off at a moment's notice. They walk in silence, all bursting with excitement, desperate to speak about what might be hidden behind that rock and what they intend to do with their share.

Stunned silence grips the boys. They stare at the wall of rock and mud in front of them.

## Chapter 14

'Oh Jesus, we're trapped.' cries Tom. His knees turning to water. 'Spider has buried us alive. This is what Blind Peter wanted, he has killed us all, we'll never get his treasure now.' 'He wasn't trying to kill us,' state's Chris, 'he was in my head remember. He just wanted the money to help the poor.' 'Well were dead now,' says Tom, but he still starts digging into the loose soil with his hands. For every handful he removes, more starts to pour in from the ceiling, until eventually Casey pulls him back. 'You're making it worse,' he says 'More and more is falling in, it'll all be on top of you if you're not careful. Let's try our phones.' Casey pulls out a sad little pay as you go. 'My old one was dead from the water. Dad went schitz. He refused to buy me another smart phone. I had to get this out of my own money.' He lights it up, but there is no signal. Tom checks his, but gets the same result. They look at Chris. 'It's still in the airing cupboard. I forgot to check to see if it was working again.'

'Do you think Spider would call the Police to rescue us?' asks Tom. 'If he knows the tunnel has caved in,' replies Casey 'I think the chances of him organising a rescue are Zero. He'll be glad we are buried. No one to grass on him and get him into trouble. He won't care if we die, so long as he doesn't get into trouble.' 'Does anyone know your here?' pleads Tom. 'Will anyone come looking for you?' 'No,' replies Casey sadly 'Spider grabbed me, I wasn't even planning to come here. What about you guys?' 'We're late back from swimming is all,' says Chris. 'The folks might have started calling round friends by now, but only Luke and Little Chris might even guess we have come back here. I don't think we can expect a rescue any time soon. Even then, they would have to dig through miles of earth. Let's try going the other way. This was a drainage channel, it's got to empty out somewhere.' 'It did,' says Tom despondently, 'It used to empty onto the beach, but the authorities blocked it up centuries ago, because it was dangerous, that's what I heard anyway.' 'Yeah, I heard the same.' says Casey, 'but I don't know where I know it from. It's got to be worth a look.  We've got nothing better to do.  If we just sit here, the batteries will run out and then we get to suffocate in the dark.'  'Thanks for the cheery thought,  It's not like I was scared enough already,' says Tom as the start trudging back down the tunnel.

  The tunnel is battered in places, much worse than the other part they have been in.  Much of the damage is recent.  They are careful to disturb these areas as little as possible.  After a few hundred yards they pass the side tunnel where the gold is hidden and the tunnel starts to slope downward.
  'It's sloping downwards,' says Chris excitedly, 'down towards the beach.'   'If there was an exit,' says Tom. 'Surely we would be able to see some light by now.'  'No.  It's probably dark out there by now.  What's the time?' asks Chris.  Casey looks at his phone.  'Eight thirty,' he answers.
  They trudge onwards, until, as Tom had pessimistically predicted, they find their way blocked.  There is a grid of iron bars set across the tunnel, similar to the ones which block the fall into the Abbots Latrine, each bar half an inch thick and solid.  Beyond that

is a wooden wall, with a heavy wooden door set into it, but through chinks in the woodwork and the gaps round the door, they can see glimmers of light and smell the mud of Southampton Water. Tom drops his back pack to the floor and whips out the hammer and chisel he had used to expose Sister Mary's remains. 'At least we have a chance of getting past this.' he says and begins whacking at the stonework around the grill. Where the mortar on the Abbot's Lodge had been hundreds of years old and had crumbled like dust, this appeared far more modern and solid. The chisel, however, did begin to do its work and within twenty minutes Tom had managed to gouge a hole around one of the bars. Despite being free though it would not move so much as an inch, held in place by the solidity of the grid as a whole. Undaunted Tom switched to the next bar up. The tunnel is six foot high. The bars are sunken into the wall every four inches. Eighteen bars sunk into each wall and nine into the floor and ceiling. A total of fifty four bars and it has taken Tom twenty minutes to make a hole around one of them. Casey, who is the best at Maths, groups the bars into threes and counts around the grid. 'It's going to take us eighteen hours to chip a hole around all the bars!' he states. 'I haven't got anything better to do.' replies Tom busy chipping away at the next bar. He completes work on the second bar and hands the tools to Casey. 'Your turn.' With Chris still holding the torch, Casey continues work. 'Do you know where this tunnel comes out,' he asks, 'someone might hear us working and come and investigate.' 'No idea,' replies Tom. 'I thought it had been collapsed and buried at this end, like the rest of you. My best bet would be somewhere between Netley Castle and Weston Sailing Club. There's a big stretch of woodland there.'

They work on for another hour. Taking turns to rest, hold the torch or chip away at the mortar and stone. They are confident, that although it will be difficult hard work, they will eventually be able to get themselves clear of the tunnels. That is, until the torch starts to fade. The faint glimmers of light through the wooden doorway had faded long ago and as the torch grows dimmer and dimmer, their moral fades with it. 'We can't work in the darkness,' says Chris, who is taking his turn with the tools.  'I already smacked my fingers twice.'  'We should be able to continue in the morning,' says Casey, 'if there is enough light coming through the doorway.'  'Have you got a light on your phone,' asks Tom,  pulling his out of his pocket.  The screen lights up and gives a minimal amount of light to work by, but flicks off after a few seconds.  Casey flicks through the crude menu system on his pay as you go and under a section marked extras finds a flashlight tool, but before he lights it up ....  'Hey, guys I have a signal.  One bar, lets ring the Police or the fire brigade.  They'll have us out of here in no time.'  but before he can dial, Tom interrupts, 'No stop.  If we call the cops, Chris and me will be in trouble for trespass and vandalism, but worse than that, they'll take the gold.'  'So who do we call,' asks Casey.  'I don't want to spend the night here.  I'm probably in trouble already for being late home.'  'You won't be in trouble when you come home with a bag full of gold coins,' answers Tom.  'Call Luke or Little Chris, or both of them.  Get them to bring hack saws and an axe to chop through the wood.'

'I think a crowbar would be better to just break the door open.' says Chris. 'I've seen Little Chris using an axe, it was a scary sight.' 'Tell them to bring backpacks as well.' says Tom. 'I'm not leaving the gold behind. We have been through too much to get it. We need to make sure the poor benefit from the gold though, otherwise, Blind Peter might be after us again.'

 Casey phones Luke. He lets it ring until the answer phone picks up. 'It's Casey, call me, it's an emergency.' He then hangs up. 'I'll send a text too, just in case.' In the mean time, Tom is phoning Little Chris. He picks up on the third ring. 'Awright.' 'Chris, it's Tom. I'm with Casey and my brother, we need your help.' 'Shit! What's happened,' asks Little Chris, using his usual vulgar expletives. 'We're stuck in the tunnels under the Abbey,' says Tom. 'There is an exit into the woods, down by Netley Castle somewhere, but it has been boarded up and has a metal grill across it. We need you and Luke to come down with hack saws and a crow bar.' 'Why don't you just call the fire brigade?' asks Little Chris. 'Because we found the gold too, so bring some back packs as well.' 'I might be a while,' answers Chris 'I'm supposed to be getting ready for bed.  Mum and Dad won't be going for a while, give me a couple of hours, I'll ring you back when I get close.'

 Chris hangs up the phone.  He is laid on his bed, fully clothed.  He had been reading, when the phone went off.  His parents usually let him read for a while before he goes to bed.  He would string it out for as long as possible, which meant his mum would be in and out for an hour or two, before she finally got him to sleep.  Chris gets his sleeping bag and other bulky stuff out of the wardrobe and shoves it under his duvet.  He grabs his back pack, tips his school books out, puts his torch in, turns the light off and sneaks out of his room.  He knows from years of experience, where all the creaky spots are in the hall and on the stairs.  He sneaks down the stairs.  The television is playing in the lounge and he can hear his parents talking over the top of it.  The front door is one of those new UPVC ones, so fortunately it opens and closes smoothly, without the slightest sound.  All his dads tools are in the garage. The up and over door at the front is locked, but he knows the door at the back never is. He goes through the side gate, also never locked because he and his older brother are always in and out of it with their bikes. Rather than put the garage light on, he flicks his torch on. The garage is a tip and hasn't seen a car for as long as Chris can remember. There is a work bench, covered in tools and leftovers from a million jobs, paint cans, off cuts of wood and spare fittings, from flat pack furniture. An old optimist sailing dinghy sits in the middle of the floor, the boys used to sail it when they were younger, but have lost interest in it. It's too small and slow for their liking now. Power boating is currently their new favourite water sport, ever since they have been allowed to take the helm of some of the Sea Scouts boats. They have since gone on to complete their RYA Level 2 powerboat drivers course and Chris has competed in the RYA Honda Youth RIB challenge. He skirts round the pile of garden furniture and the lawnmower and searches through the debris on the work bench. Eventually he comes up with a hack saw and a junior hacksaw, which both have metal blades in them. He looks through the draws

on the front of the bench and finds spare
blades for both.  He can't find a crowbar, or
an axe, but eventually settles for a claw
hammer, which he hopes will do the job.
After dropping all the equipment into his
back pack, he switches the torch off and
drops that in too.  He pushes his bike to the
garage door.  The sky is clear, but there is no
moon, he knows that once he is clear of the
street lights, it will be dark. Little Chris quickly
collects his bike lights from a shelf and clips
them in place.  He has already had one set
nicked when he left the bike outside the
shops, so rarely leaves them on the bike.   He
doesn't turn the lights on as he pushes the
bike out the garden gate, carefully latching
the gate behind him to ensure it does not
blow around and bring his dad out.

Chris cycles round the empty streets of the
estate.  It reminds him of the film with Will
Smith, where he is the last man alive on the
planet, everyone else having been turned
into ravaging Zombies.  His nerves are
starting to get the better of him by the time
he has to take a cut way through a stretch of
woods known as the buffer zone.  It's literally

just a narrow stretch of woodland running between two parts of the estate, with a footpath running up the middle.  Little Chris jumps at every shadow, glancing nervously from side to side, his bike is wobbling all over the place.  He considers turning back and going the long way round, but if he does, he might miss Luke, if the others have got hold of him and he is on the way.  This is the way Luke would come to get to his house, so this is the way he must go.  There is one street light at the halfway point of the pathway, so Little Chris focuses on that and keeps pedalling.  He reaches the light, but it has destroyed his night vision.  He can see very little beyond it.  He stops under the light, gazing up the darkened path beyond, waiting for his vision to improve, when he sees the figure.  It is stood off to the side of the path, hiding under a tree, watching him.  Little Chris pauses, waiting to see if it will move, waiting to see if it is just a trick of his imagination or a mugger lying in wait.  He remembers his Mum warning him about a dog walking pensioner, who had been mugged walking along this path after dark.  He did not remember, whether the mugger had actually been caught, or whether this was him waiting for another victim in the dark.

## Chapter 15

'Chris.' whispers the shadowy figure. Oh my god. The mugger knows his name. In a panic he starts to wheel his bike round, hoping to get away before the mugger can catch him. 'Chris, It's me, Luke.'

Relief floods through him. He has never been so glad to see his friend before in his life. 'Am I glad to see you,' he says, 'I was crapping my pants back there, I thought you were the mugger.' They compare equipment. Luke also has a torch and hack saw, but no crowbar or axe either.

They decide to put their bike lights on and follow the main roads to get to Netley. Neither of them fancy the dark ride through the country park, even though it is significantly shorter. Within twenty minutes, they arrive outside the main gate of the Abbey ruins, on Abbey Hill road. The road runs on down to Weston shore. The Abbey Gate it to their right as they sit on the road, a driveway down to Netley Castle is on the left. A signpost reads, Netley Castle, Private. But just a few yards down this private road is a track leading off to the right, with another sign reading Weston Shore Link. 'Looks like they put a new cycle track through the woods,' says Luke, 'Bonus,' replies Little Chris and they head down it until they are out of sight of the road.

  Then Little Chris pulls up. 'We need to phone the others back,' he says as he pulls out his mobile. Chris does last number re-dial and Casey picks up instantly. 'You took your time,' he says. 'Get over it,' replies Chris, 'We're helping you out here.' 'Whereabouts are you,' asks Casey. Little Chris explains their location and tells Casey what tools they have brought with them. 'That's good mate,' answers Casey. 'We're going to start banging on the bars at the end of the tunnel, see if you can hear it.'

  Casey takes the hammer and starts whacking the bars with all his might. Chris can hear it from down the phone, even when he holds it away from his ear. He hangs up the phone and keeps listening. 'They're banging on the bars, but I can't hear a thing. Let's cycle further down the path.' They continue on until they have reached the open fields alongside the Weston Sailing Club. Then they cut across the fields down to the shore.  Chris phones Casey back.  'We've been all the way along the path and we're down by the shore now.  Have you been banging all the time.'  Casey confirms that they had never stopped.  'Well keep doing it, we'll cut back along the shore path and keep listening.'  Luke and Little Chris head back towards Netley Castle, the sea is to their right.  There is a little stone built sea wall running along the shoreline, probably there to protect the footpath from high tides. There are rarely any significant waves this far up Southampton Water.  The path is little more than a dirt track.  Little Chris leads, with Luke following behind.  They listen carefully, but all they can hear is the lap of waves against the shore.  The only excitement, is when they come to a low muddy dip in the path, where the wall has failed.  The only way around is to climb over the wall and walk along the beach for a few yards, the tide not being particularly high that night.  To their left, the boggy patch stretches right up to the edge of the woodland, where a wire fence blocks entry.

Instead of climbing over the wall, Little Chris decides to climb onto it and then drag is bike along over the mud and water.  It works and neither he or the bike gets particularly muddy, so Luke repeats the trick.  Eventually, the path pitches up on the shoreline below the Castle.  The castle was originally one of Henry VIII's fortifications, but it had been extensively modified and changed over the years.  It's most famous occupant hand been Colonel Chrichton.  The boys know this because he was responsible for starting the rival sea scout troop in Netley.  The boys had regularly raced against Sir Harry Chrichton's own Sea Scouts on many occasions, usually at the Netley Regatta where they beat them at rowing.  The castle had then been a convalescent home and now had been turned into private apartments, worth millions.

  'The exit must be somewhere in the bottom half of those woods,' says Luke.  'Remember it was a drainage channel to wash sewage down to Southampton Water.  The lowest place along the path, was where the mud was, so let's head up into the woods from there.  They head back along the path and ditch their bikes, just before they reach the muddy bit.  They push the bikes right up against the six foot wire fence along the edge of the woods and then use them to help climb over.  They follow the fence back towards the swampy muddy bit and then start skirting it round to the right and higher up the hill into the woods, where the ground dries out, and all that is left is a trickle of water running along the bottom of a narrow gully.  They follow the channel up the hill.  The water dries out completely, but the ditch continues.  Then they hear the ringing sound of metal on metal and start sprinting up the hill as fast as they can.  The noise is coming from within a dense thicket of trees and bushes, which the boys have to push and scramble and eventually crawl, to get through.

  In the middle of the thicket, densely overgrown, so that only the odd stone is poking through, is revealed the arched stone entrance to a tunnel.  Within this archway is the wooden wall described by Casey.  It has faded green paint, which is cracked and pealing to expose grey weathered and rotting wood beneath.  There is a small doorway in the centre, only about four foot high, which is secured by a padlock.  It is the biggest oldest padlock they have ever seen, with a hey hole in the front, rather than the bottom.  It is so rusted, it looks like it will never open again.  The boys bang hard against the wall with both hands.  'We're here. We're here. You can stop.'  The noise ceases and they hear cheering from within.  Little Chris pulls his hammer out.  He stands with feet wide apart, like he has been trained to use an axe, grips the hammer with both hands and swings at the lock.  Despite being old and rusty, the lock remains firmly closed.  He strikes again and again, to no avail, until eventually he notices the hasp has started to part company with the wood of the wall.  He alternates between using the claw to lever the hasp away from the wood and bashing it with the hammer.  When he gets tired, Luke takes over.  His superior size and strength makes the difference and the hasp falls away.

Luke pulls the door open, 'Your knight in shining armour has arrived,' he jokes.  There is a gap of about four foot between the wooden wall and the metal grill, Little Chris steps into the tunnel mouth beside him and they both drop their back packs to the floor and start pulling out hack saws. They figure that cutting through just eight bars, will make a square hole big enough for them to squeeze through one at a time. The junior hacksaw is pretty ineffective and there is not really enough room for three of them to cut at the same time anyway, but with one person working from each side they have a hole cut within twenty minutes. When the metal grid finally drops to the floor there is much hugging and celebrating.

 'Let's see the treasure then,' says Little Chris. 'It's back up the tunnel.' says Tom. 'We left it there until we could get free.' The five boys head back up the tunnel Tom leading the way, with Little Chris's torch, Luke brings up the rear with his.

 With two hammers and a chisel working, they quickly pull a rock loose. Gold coins pour like a waterfall from the gap created. The boys carefully pull every gold coin from the hole in the wall, they eventually have to widen the hole to get to the remainder and pull bits of rotten chest out of the way. They have four back packs between them. The gold coins, spread between the four bags are just about lift able. Casey, who does not have a bag helps the others lift theirs in place. They head back down to the shore, to collect the two bikes, but Casey points out, that they are so damn rich now, they can buy whatever bike they want.

 'No point in wasting a good bike though,' replies Little Chris. Tom rings his dad. After listening to his dads tirade about staying out late without permission and worrying him to death, Tom persuades him to come and collect them. His dad has a taxi van, which he uses for airport runs, so it will fit all five boys and the two bikes. Tom doesn't tell him about the gold.

 Their taxi arrives fifteen minutes later. The twins dad opens the door, but before he can start going ballistic again, the boys show him a handful of gold. 'Is that real,' is his first response. He is totally gob smacked. He picks over the coins, holding them up to the light biting them. 'How many of these have you got,' he asks, astounded, when they pat the four jingling bags.

  Casey, Luke and Little Chris, all live in the College estate in Hamble.  Luke's house is the most central, so they head for there and the others ring their parents, taking some time, to explain why they are out and where they are and what is happening.  Eventually each parent agrees to come and collect them from Luke's house.  The twins dad phones their mum and tells her to meet them all as well.

  The boys pour the gold coins out onto the coffee table in the centre of Luke's lounge. As each set of parents arrive they express their astonishment and the boys launch into numerous jumbled explanations of how and where they found it.  Eventually, the Police are called and a more logical and sequential explanation is provided, as the young constable prompts and probes and asks all the relevant questions and insists that only one person talks at a time.  Although the boys do their best to avoid any mention of ghosts, they do include Blind Peter as the reason for Spider and Bugsy's flight.  Bugsy gets dug out of the tunnels by the fire brigade later that night.

Eventually, the Constable explains, that to the best of his knowledge, treasure, belongs to the land owner of the piece of land where it was discovered, though the finders, generally get a portion of the value of the find.  Until ownership of the treasure and its value can be established he decides that it should be homed at the local police station.

After counting the coins into secure leather bags, he provides five receipts, each for 206 gold coins, a fifth share of the total find.  Over the next few days, the Police visit the site of the find, with surveyors and establish that the exact site of the find is situated under unregistered land, which may have originally been part of Colonel Chrichton's estate, but which was fenced off, to prevent access to the tunnels.  When the estate was sold off, the title of the land sold, did not include the fenced off portion, which fell into disuse and disrepair.  Therefore, the state would claim the treasure, offering it to museums, but give the finders, the full market value of the find.  About two million pounds each!

  In order to ensure that Blind Peter does not bother them again, they agree to donate half their find to charity.  English Heritage gets a million, to build a proper visitor centre at the Abbey, where Blind Peters Diary is put on display.  Sir Harry Chrichtons Own, 4th Netley Sea Scouts get a million, to build a new hq, Hamble Sea Scouts, TS Mercury Group, get a million, Cancer research UK get a million and finally, the boys schools share a million.

  The boys, along with English Heritage organise a funeral at St Edwards church, for Sister Mary.  The vicar says the usual prayers and homilies and the boys tell the true story of Blind Peter and Sister Mary, to the congregation.  They have kept their side of the bargain and are relieved to think that they are now safe from the blind monks ghost.

  It is high summer.  The millionaires, they each have a trust fund which they can access with their parents agreement, have all bought a small rigid inflatable powerboat, which they keep at Mercury Marina.   They have been out racing the boats up and down Southampton Water and have now pulled into Hamble Quay, to buy lunch at the Blue Star Cafe.  The sun is shining, it is twenty five degrees and they have chips and ice cream for lunch.  They are all sitting talking about their adventures, when a hand appears from behind, snatching a tray of chips out of Casey's hand.

The boys turn to see a dishevelled looking Spider, shovelling chips into his mouth.  'You owe me big time boys.  You stole my treasure.  I want a million quid, or believe me, I will be making your life a misery.'  He jabs his greasy finger into Casey's face to emphasis his point.


'I don't think so spider.'  It's Chris speaking, 'You're going to walk away from here.  You're going to leave this village and never return. You will never speak to us again and you will never do anything to harm any one of us or our families.  In fact Spider, you're going to turn over a new leaf.  You're going to be polite friendly and helpful to everyone you meet and then I might just let you live.'

Spider is staring at Chris, his mouth agape. The other boys turn to see Chris's eyes burning with flame. 'Yes sir,' says Spider as he turns and sprints away across the quay.

## Afterword

The principal characters in this book are loosely based on real people of the same name. The twins dad claims his back garden does not look like a building site, but his wife disagreed, so the comment stayed in the book.

It is possible to visit Netley Abbey and many of the other places mentioned in the book. The tunnels in the Abbey do exist, but I have never been in them, apart from when I was asked to help clear the rubbish from the visible section. This was before we entered the age of health and safety.

There is no visible exit from the tunnels, but there is regularly water still flowing through the channels, so it must flow somewhere. The latrine behind the Abbot's Lodge is no longer connected to the tunnel system and is full of water, so it appears there has been some kind of collapse. I would strongly advise my readers not to emulate the boys in the story as I wouldn't want to be held responsible for anyone stuck in a cave in.

The legend of Blind Peter is well known in the area, along with the deaths of Slone and the builder.   I don't believe that these tales have any basis in fact and may have been invented during the 1800s.  So your chances of finding any treasure in the tunnels is not good.

Made in the USA
Charleston, SC
01 July 2014